Unworthy

L. Marie Wood

Contents

Other L. Marie Wood titles

<u>*The Realm Trilogy*</u>

The Realm

Cacophony-The Realm, Book 2

Accursed-The Realm, Book 3

Other Titles

The Unholy Trinity

12 Hours

Mars, The Band Man, and Sara Sue

Crescendo

Telecommuting

The Black Hole

The Open Book

Tales of Time

The Promise Keeper

Non-Fiction Titles

The Horror Aesthetic: Essays from the Dark Corner of the Genre

About Horror: The Study and Craft

Acknowledgments

Thank you, Sean, Bree, and Mike, for helping me find pockets of time to do this thing I love.

Thank you, Laura Fasching and MaryAnn David, for your keen eyes along this journey.

Thank you, readers, for travelling along this road with me.

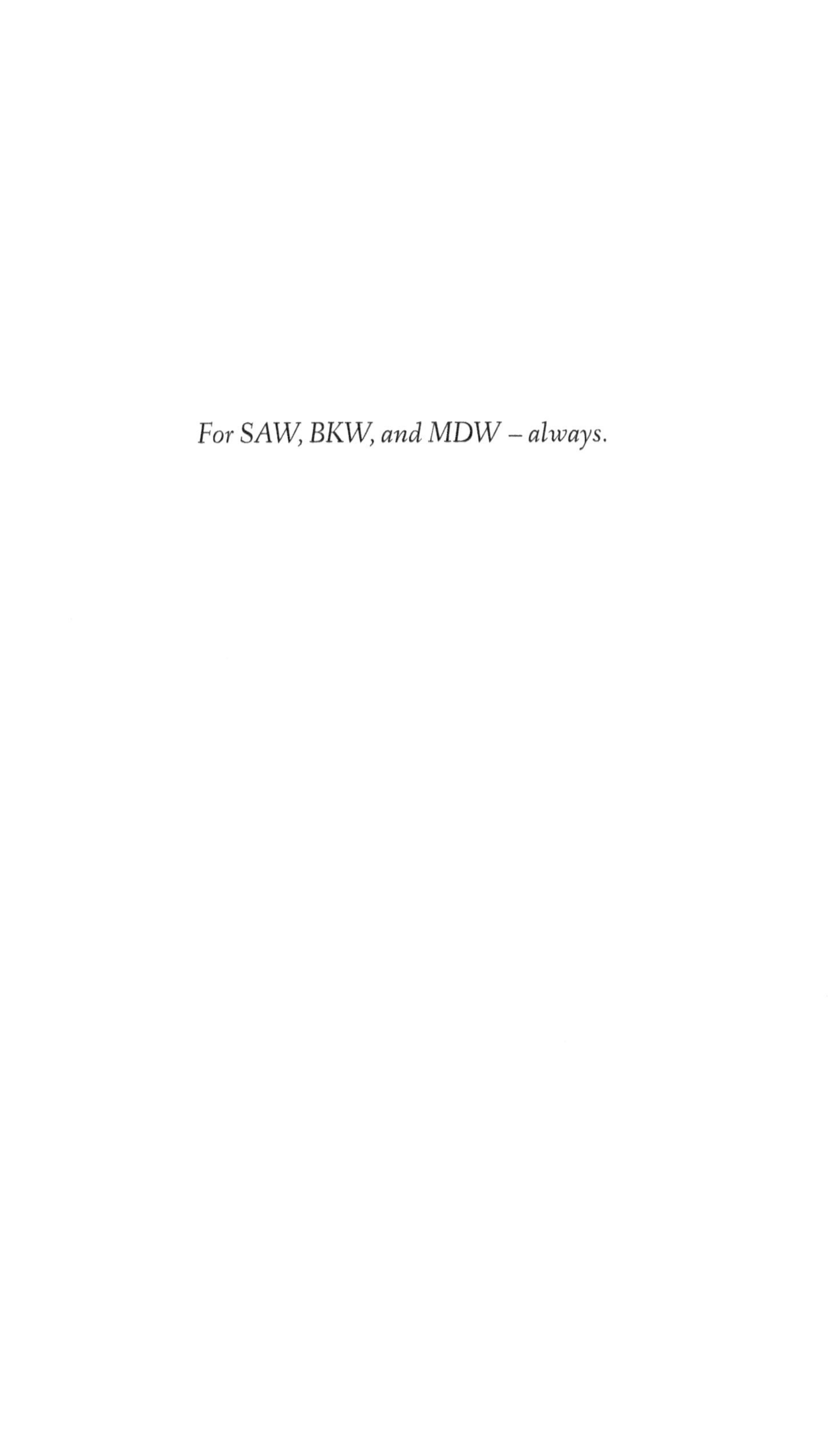

For SAW, BKW, and MDW – always.

Unworthy: A Fiction

At the right angle, under the proper lens, the real path is shown, paved with bones and held in place by the viscid and the bloody. There the truth is told, spoken in whispers into ruined ears. There, smiles sit askew on bloated faces, waiting for their turn on the other side of the veil.

NEXT
Part One

Loud.

So loud when he left, the door slamming behind him, echoing throughout the room, bouncing from one side to the other of my head, my brain, my soul.

Gone.

Gone because his job is done.

It is over for him, and he can leave, can run, can distance himself from this forever if he chooses to, really.

But for me, it has just begun.

She looks so pretty there, with her hair haloing her head, brown and thick, curly, glossy.

Healthy.

Liar.

He left without saying anything, nothing at all, actually, not even as she spoke her frustrations, choosing then, then, even then to tell him how she felt. How he failed her. How beneath her he was.

How base.

Fine.

That was her choice.

But didn't he know that I was here? Sure, he did – he saw me at her hem, small there where I had never been small before. He saw me, yet he still left, and that, well, that is fine. It has to be. What else can it be now?

The door boomed when he left. Could she hear it where she was?

Where is she?

What is she now that all of this is said and her armor has been laid down, battlement left unguarded?

What am I?

White and gold.

And red.

Her velvet, saturated through, dark red against the wine.

Makes brown.

Like a stain.

Gold bangles to accent skin that won't be the same tomorrow, today, ever again.

He left me there to watch still set and gray color with the hope that osmosis, proximity, divine clarity showed itself between these gilded walls.

Coward.

Bring forth the bejeweled cup and drinketh yourself, you bastard.

Perhaps she had been right about him all along.

Her hair is splayed so beautifully on the floor. Gold and purple hair tinsel, thin as filament, threaded through, spiraling delicately among the strands: the identity of the royal. So like my own, but more in every way... more prevalent, more vibrant, more deserved. I touch my own strands, find the tinsel and pull, but it doesn't come, honey's paste secure and the practitioner talented as they are expected to be considering the coif upon which they work.

My ringed fingers twitch, unsure what to touch next.

The eyes of the seer to see.

The tongue of the speaker to speak.

Pray tell which first? Which not at all?

Legs cramped beneath my frock, but still I sit as I am destined to do. My place here is written and I shall not move unless struck down.

But for how long?

How long am I to sit here as I feel, not moving a muscle, feeling my limbs turn to stone, grow cold as the floor, cold as rock, cold as she?

How long?

The books were never read, my lady, the rules never navigated. When does the sexton mark the death knell?

Cold.

Chill in the air from the window open to the world. Cold outside as it is within. Even Mother Nature bends to her will.

Silent.

Quiet as death.

Death outside.

Death inside.

Blood on the ground.

Blood on the floor.

Seeping, pooling, sinking, congealing, permeating, invading, red, red, red death the final and I see, I see I see it from here, I see it, I tell you, I see it all.

Sight to blind me.

Sight to school me.

Predator, you fiend, I know you well.

Spare one or none, I no longer care because the tinsel in her hair stays firm even when they would rot out before long, rot out by the heat of the sun. Rot out because rot it must as she no longer is.

But then who is next?

He left because he was supposed to. Prince that he was, from a family outside of the province. Never given a proper title, and oh, did it anger him. 'Twas a girl that was born and only one such that he could not kill to take the throne. Ah yes, he left because he cannot stay. And that is fine as well.

I shed my rings. They are of no use to me now.

Imperial Topaz cut in the shape of her mother's tears sitting in the finest Indian gold. Too big for my finger, but I feel it grip me as it slides easily down, slick with blood.

And I sit.

The hills beyond are green in the spring when life buds anew all over the land. I see them now, and though they should be covered with grass and flowers that I might pick and bring home for her to smell, to see, to love, they are brown to my veiled eyes. Though life abounds there, I see death, can feel the soil littered with bodies and choking on the blood that waters it relentlessly, forcing it to drink, to fill to the brim, to die along with the one that cultivated it. Go on, then. Die as you might, fickle grass. I shall never see your beauty again, not even the innocence of a tulip will sway my eye. Should I ever get up to see you clearly again, that is. Therefore, it matters not if you die or do not.

Mouth open.

My mouth is open.

Her mouth is open.

Breath tickles my nose.

What comes from the open mouth when the speaker has lost their voice?

Over that hill is the town named for her father's father, or so the story goes. He was beloved there, a soldier who had saved the town from conquer. In his honor, they named it so to remember him by, painted his likeness, and put it on the map.

People care about us, she said.

Then where are they?

I sit.

I wait.

The sun dips behind the hill that marks my territory, and I wait.

Where are these people that care for us so much? Where is the one who should be here to decide what comes next but cannot?

The queen is silenced, I want to yell but know that I should not, because it isn't true, is it?

No, the queen is not silenced, is she? Because she...

The people of old made it so that people could eat, she used to say. Right over that hill stood tall buildings, bridges, and motorized cars. They went to work every day, buying and selling, creating and testing, giving and taking. They had more money than they knew what to do with and spent it all, letting it flow from their hands, their pockets, their bank accounts, like water running from a tap, greed the font. They laughed gaily throughout the night and woke up ill but did it all over again at every week's end. There was theater and there was shopping, and there were sporting events to rival our own. The rich were so very rich, and the poor in some places could fund an existence for the downtrodden we were accustomed to. But then he died, and the world stopped.

It froze.

It waited.

It waited for someone to say something, do something. Take over. Take charge. Take initiative.

But the ones who would do so were dead, and the town sank to its knees.

Money burned.

Towers burned.

People burned.

My family left.

Came over the hill and fortified the land to protect them from anyone else who would do so after them.

They waited.

They watched.

The shots in the night used to be numerous, Mother said. And this is what her mother had told her when she was a child. But by the time my mother was old enough to listen for them herself, they were gone. The sounds of the night, the low, wailing hum that accompanied every moment of every day in their beautiful valley, the only sound that was ever heard. And you never heard it, not really. Because it was always there, it was part of the background as much as the zebras that graze in the fields were.

Until it was gone.

Then all you could hear was the absence of it.

Nothingness.

What's over the hill now, Mama?

What do you see, Mama?

Nothing.

Corset too tight.

Mine or hers to loosen first?

Ankle twisted beneath her as she fell, broken bone pressing against skin.

Black and blue.

Bruised when blood flowed.

My ankle aches, bent awkwardly beneath heavy, motionless girth.

Must I mirror or can I move to prevent the ruin, Mama?

Must I be...

... Mama?!?

Flies buzzing overhead.

Flies with little legs that land on anything, everything. Legs with spiked hairs on them, barbed hairs that catch bits and pieces of whatever they land on and take it with them. Pollen, dander, feces. Carried to and fro, clinging to them as the flies buzzed overhead, looking for something new to land on.

I hate flies.

I hate bugs.

I hate their very nature to invade personal space, claiming everything in the world for their own if only for a second, a moment in time. Nasty, dirty, despicable things that carry disease, germs, the blood of enemies, the blood of...

Buzz.

Buzz.

Buzz.

Lands.

Lands on her face.

Rubs its legs together while sitting on her cheek.

Walks into her eye.

I want to swat it away.

Shouldn't I swat it away?

Did she swat away the flies that landed in her mother's eyes? Her father's?

Laying eggs.

I am sure the fly is laying eggs in her eye, and they will fester there, safe, warm, and protected until they hatch. And they'll hatch before the pyre, won't they? Hatch just before she is placed upon it so that all can see the movement beneath the sheet, so that all can imagine them crawling, wriggling free, stretching their newfound wings, rubbing their feet together to rid them of her viscosity.

Twelve hours... maybe 24.

Soon.

She told me of the day her mother was stung by a bee. How she passed out when they took out the stinger and didn't wake up for days, months, years. I was six then and had just swatted a bee when my mother told me that and I cried and cried, afraid the bee and his whole bee family would come after me for all my days, never letting me rest until they had all stung me to sleep.

Twelve bees... maybe 24.

Life.

Death.

She doesn't blink when the fly dances on her eye so I blink for her.

She told me I would one day wear the finest silks and lace. I would trot out a handsome man to take as my partner while I sat on the throne. She said I would be ready for love but not ready to lead when my time came, but that it wouldn't matter. I answered no, that time would never come because men were all bores, especially the pretty ones. And as for leading, well, on that account, she was right. I would bid her goodnight if only to play along with her rhyme. But she always *tsked tsked* me as I spoke and told me she knew more than I did.

Indeed.

I am not ready.

Not ready for love nor ready to lead.

There is no handsome man to stand by the side of my throne. My intended has no interest in the trivialities of the throne. He would rather hunt and gather, go over the hill and make money to bring back to his garden to bury at night. My intended does not know he is my intended at all. He does not know how I watch him as he goes on his travels, reading his commentary of the world so close but yet so far.

Parasocial.

Paranormal.

Parasomnia.

I talk to him while I'm asleep.

He looks like he hears because he smiles and laughs and oh, when he smiles, I can't help but smile too because she had it right on that score, she knew what she was talking about when she said he'd be that, for sure.

Pretty.

So very pretty.

And when he smiles, he lights up the room, and his eyes squint and his face glows.

Eye candy.

And when he laughs, he can't breathe and his body leans to the side and you hold your breath because all you want to do is laugh too but you don't know if you should because he doesn't know you doesn't see you doesn't hear you doesn't get you but oh, he is laughing again and I can't stop watching.

He likes blue, and I like him, so I watch him laugh and chuckle along quietly alongside him from across the kingdom, wondering if he notices. Lots of girls choose him, but he will choose me because I am perfect for him because he is perfect to me.

He is so pretty when he smiles.

My giggle is so loud, it is deafening, but so quiet I wonder if he can hear.

He will stand beside me as I sit on the throne that is mine, mine, rightfully mine. And he will smile so pretty, and the kingdom will adore him because he looks like he should be adored, and they will throw flowers at his feet, and he will give them all to me because it is me that he serves and will serve forever.

Can you see him, Mama?

Can you see me and him?

I will leave the castle and live by the beach because I love the water, and that is where I want to be. The kingdom will be there, and they will throw rose petals at my feet as I walk along the sand. I will kick at the water, and it will tickle my toes in retribution because it loves me, and I love it and it is mine and mine alone. And that is how I will spend my days kicking at the water and watching movies in the sky.

Tell me, Mama, tell me what I am to do now that a skin has formed on your blood as it grows cold there on the white, staining the white, marring it forever and always?

Do I cast out those who would not fight for me?

Do I make my first decree, say something pertinent, something important, something you would never say but that you have already said long ago when you were young, and it didn't matter?

Do I call for my love to be by my side because he is mine and not hers, mine and always has been, mine forever?

Perhaps.

But after.

Once my legs no longer feel attached to my body and they are as cold as ice.

Once the sun dips down past the hill and the lights turn on on the other side to glow in the sky.

Once the fly is done playing in your eye and leaves to light on something else.

I once impaled a moth on a toothpick.

I watched it as it wriggled, the throes of death short and sweet.

I showed the toothpick to my mother, as she was the only one I thought would look at it and truly see the beauty. She said I should not make it suffer so unless the other moths saw and understood.

Did the moths see and understand? Should I open the chamber and let them pass, giving the queen a wide berth as they looked on, the message hanging before them like a neon sign?

What was the message?

For whom was it written?

I will trail my finger in her blood later and scribe along the white to make matters clear.

I will write it on my body so that I remember too.

War paint.

Tribal markings engraved deep in the skin, deep in the soul.

Contouring.

Mask donned, removable, not removed.

She told me once about a tattoo she had that no one knew about. A small thing that looked like a blemish to anyone who might get close enough to see it.

I want to see it.

I want to see it now.

The queen is dead and I want to see it.

I am the queen and I want to see it.

I think I shall get one of my own once I know who I am.

I think I shall hide it in the manner of a queen.

My decree: all queens shall get a tattoo that they hide for the rest of their days.

Is that good enough, Mama?

He is back but I want him to leave.

He is here to light the torches but I want the darkness.

The white glows against it like a fluorescent. The red is as black as tar.

"Go," I tell him, "for I have not learned all yet. There is more she can give me."

I can feel his concern from here, but I do not move. I do not turn my head. I do not shift.

He does not come closer.

The blood has long ago been cut off from my leg.

Numb feels like something.

Numb feels like nothing.

Nothing hurts.

She told me once to stop doing something if it hurt, but I didn't listen. I did it anyway. I flapped my hand back and forth until my wrist felt it might break; I forced my legs into a split when they didn't want to go.

I stared at the sun even though she told me not to.

It showed me black dots.

It showed me death.

Her blood on white, black as midnight.

My blood.

"Do you see?" I asked the unfortunate who was volunteered to stick her head and look upon us. "She lies so peacefully."

The woman wants to say something but knows she shouldn't. I could have her tongue if she spoke words I found distasteful. Mother would not have liked that. Mother would not have done that, but I am not mother, cannot be mother, will never be mama. And so, she is silent because she knows what is good for her.

Be kind and rewind.

Her mother played hopscotch with mine as children. She thinks that matters to me.

And it does.

If you do the crime, you do the time.

They played hand-clapping games on park benches, thick paint, soft from so many coats, covering splintered wood.

Miss Mary Mack Mack Mack
all dressed in black black black
with silver buttons buttons buttons
all down her back back back

She thinks that matters to me.
And it does.
Mama smiled when I missed.
I smiled too.
Maybe we will go over the hill together, my pretty thing and me. Maybe he will put me on his back and carry me over it, and we'll never come back.
Maybe she was the last queen.
Maybe the queen has decided to call it done.

But then where would they get their grain? Their hay? Their wood?

Where would they sing their songs or drink ale as they pleased after a long day in the fields?

What would they do?

What if everyone over here followed me over there, crowding in, dimming the beautiful lights that light up the sky with their numbers?

What would she think when the kingdom was chewed up and spit out?

My hair would be long and straight, pink and purple and turquoise and blue.

I would have lost the gold; it wouldn't have mattered anymore.

And what of it?

What could she do?

She couldn't reprimand me, send me to my room, banish me to the badlands, make me live with the crows. She couldn't ground me, take my access, forbid me to watch my pretty as he goes to the restaurants, the movies, the park making everyone turn their heads, smile at him and hope he deigns to return it. I'd still see him because he'd be on the other side of the hill in my hand, rubbing shoulders with those who walk the sidewalks and wear sundresses and shorts. He'd be there with lights illuminating his face while glasses clanked and silverware clinked against plates. I could speak to him while he ate, his bite my bite because he made it so, showing me everything because he knows I would love it as much as he does. She couldn't stop me even if she could try.

But she can't.

Try.

She couldn't do any of that because the red is on the white and it is black like the night.

She can't even swat the fly away from her eyes.

One hundred billion stars and she sees every one of them.

Tell me, do they gleam? Do they shimmer, Mama? Or are they muted and cold, burnt out?

Do I want to know?

A shadow crawls across the floor, and I hear my breath retreat into my mouth. A new day is dawning outside, and the people over the hill are waking, stretching, yawning.

The house is awake because the queen is awake.

I sit looking at the ring... her ring... my ring and know that my leg will work when I move it from under my body, heavy with responsibility. I know that she has told me everything I needed to know and that I have heard it all.

I know that she is dead.

He comes to the room tentatively again, footsteps outside the door pacing, waiting, milling until I bid him enter. He looks tired, and I know that he will step back. I know that he wants to step back. Leading had never been the thing that he wanted. He had been her handsome man, standing next to her while she sat on her throne. And now that she was dead, he would be happy to let the next man come in to perform the duty that was no longer his. And that was fine.

"I rise, Father," I say, but he doesn't hear me. I move to stand but my legs don't obey. I look at the sky and notice the clouds forming. The pyre will be pretty on this gray day.

"What you want you already have, child," he says without saying it, eye cascading over me again as they had yesterday.

He does not look at her.

He does not see what I saw move under my gaze.

He does not see...

He leaves again, a heavy sigh causing him to shiver as he walks away from her, away from me... away.

Perhaps, dear father, you were right after all.

Daylight comes, and I can no longer bear to look at her.

She told me this moment would come, and here it is. But I cry anyway because I can feel the door closing, the page turning. I can feel my growing pains as she told me I used to as a child, can feel myself growing larger even as she grows smaller. Her light extinguished, and body changed. And it hurts, and it is real, and I cry. I cry for myself. I cry for her. I cry for the queen.

I hope it pleases her that I now know the steps are my own, just as it was for hers. Her journey was unique, as mine will be, and my beginning was epic and noteworthy in its silence, in its bloody residue. As I come out on the other side of the night, that was to be the last as I knew it with the common eyes I was so desperate to keep, clarity has been granted. She could no more have helped me than I will help mine when the time comes.

She told me once that I was formidable, and I believe that now. She said the others weren't ready, that their fates and follies would come to bear in succession when the tide turned, and that it was me who could withstand anything. She said I would rise, their bodies, to a number, aground like litter at my feet. She made clear through every trial, that it was me who would survive all, even the horror of night. And she was right. The red on white, so clean and pure, is proof of that.

PATTY

Patty cowered in the corner, unsure of what to do. She could hear him coming but felt stupid running away. She didn't know what kind of mood he was in; she never did. Maybe he felt like hitting her, maybe he felt like insulting her, maybe he felt like shouting obscenities, or maybe he would only stare at her in disgust. She didn't know which scenario was worse. Every time she thought she was seeing him at his angriest, he would come back with two times the intensity. She never knew what to expect, and it frightened her. He'd stomp around the house and throw things at the wall. He'd make a whole lot of noise, but that wasn't the scary part. Nor was the endless yelling and shouting and harping and belaboring. He was the master of beating a dead horse. But none of that was what frightened her. It was the look in his eyes that really got to her. A silent, slow-burning hatred that had been there for years, growing more intense every day.

She wondered if she saw it there—that look—when they

were dating. It may have been there from the beginning, but in her love-struck ignorance, she might have missed it. There was always some major fault he saw in her, even then. If it wasn't the way she chewed her food, it was the way she dressed. If it wasn't the way she dressed, then it was the way she walked. If it wasn't this, it was that. There would always be something that he didn't like, couldn't stand, didn't know if he could live with. He never said that kind of stuff outright back then. He would allude to not liking a particular outfit, or hairstyle. Of course, being in love and wanting desperately to please her mate, she would change her hairstyle or give away the dress that he didn't like to make him happy. She was determined not to let anything come between them, especially something that she could easily rectify. As time went on, though, there were things that he didn't like that she couldn't change, like her voice, or her height. Little things. Things that sound almost comical when you hear them. He didn't like the way her voice took on a rich alto glide, kind of like the sexy voice of Anita Baker. He thought she sounded too much like a man. Patty would joke that he should have asked another woman to marry him; maybe Olive Oil would do the trick. She never forgot the icy cold look he gave her at that remark.

Another thing she would never forget was what happened the weekend before they got married. Two days before the wedding, they drove to Hampton to meet up with his parents. She was so excited. She and her soon-to-be mother-in-law went off in their own little corner of the house to whisper about the upcoming events. They settled in the next room and cracked the door open so that they would be able to hear if one of 'the boys' was trying to sneak a peek and listen to what they were saying. A couple of minutes later, voices that were both boisterous and joyous emitted from the other room. At first, she wasn't paying attention to them. She was engrossed in the fantasy of her upcoming wedding. But the sudden drop in tone made her listen. She didn't know at the time what was making her eavesdrop, but she knew that she had to do it. Something was making her do it. She heard her fiancé say to his father the phrase that lingers in her mind to this day, almost two years later. She heard her soon-to-be husband say,

"Dad, I'm not sure I'm doing the right thing here. I mean, I'm just so tired of her bullshit that I don't know if I should do this. Look at her! She's the most plain-Jane girl I've ever seen in my life!"

She remembered standing there, her feet glued in place, in shock. She had been thinking that, in the next few days, she was going to have the best day of her life. That's what every woman thinks of their wedding day. She was going to marry the man she loved more than anything in the world. She hadn't listened to that little voice in her head, the one that told her she was ugly and stupid, mediocre and simple. She had ignored that little voice, the one that whispered things to her at all the wrong moments. The one that told her what to do and how to behave. The one that she usually trusted. That little voice in her head told her that she wouldn't be allowed to have a fairy-tale wedding, or a fairy-tale life, for that matter. It told her that no one would ever love her the way she thought they should. No one. But she didn't believe it. She thought things would be different. Like her mother used to say, when she was sober, that was, 'That's what you get for thinking.'

As she sat dumbfounded next to her soon-to-be mother-in-law, who was pretending she didn't hear anything, Patty scolded herself. 'It shouldn't have been a shock', that mysterious, cynical, mean-spirited voice chimed in her head, the sentiment seeming to reverberate from ear to ear. 'You were forewarned.' Still, she couldn't believe it.

She was crushed. His words put her in tears. She explained them as premarital jitters when his mother asked her what was wrong. *Could she really have not heard?* His mother seemed genuine in her concern. Patty began to doubt herself then, like she always did. *Did I hear what I think I heard?*

Patty decided to lie down upstairs. She told herself that she heard him incorrectly. That it really was just a case of premarital jitters, and it was making her misconstrue his words. She talked herself into believing that everything was fine. It was an easy notion to accept when you factored in his behavior later. He hugged and kissed her in front of all his high school buddies that night, acting like the happy groom-to-be. He seemed proud to take her as his wife. So, she talked herself into believing that her ears had played a trick on her earlier. He cuddled up as close to her as he could that night, and when they made love, when he made love to her, it was proof that he truly loved her, deep in his heart. And more than that, it proved that he was *attracted* to her. That's what she told herself. That's what she made herself believe. But over the months, through all the apologies, after all the roses had died, and after all the chocolate had melted, her mind's eye started allowing the rest of her to see what he was about. It revealed all the memories she had thrown in a mental lockbox, like the way he had dominated her since the very beginning, and how he never considered her wellbeing in any situation. It was always all about him. The resurrection of these memories jarred her flowery sense of contentment. It jerked her into reality. It prompted her to do something about it. It prompted her to make a move.

He had a sharp temper. Sometimes he would come home and wage a verbal war with her for no apparent reason. He was quick, cold, and cutting. He knew all of her weak spots and how to push all of her buttons. It was like sport for him. He would come home and insult her about anything: how she kept the house, or how she kept herself—let the games begin. A game that only he could win. One way or another.

Patty tried to retaliate, to talk back, to stand up for herself. But none of that worked. He just ate it up. He said he liked a woman who would show a little spunk now and then. He told her that she never struck him as that kind of woman, but he welcomed her little outbursts. He would say that just before he smacked her into a wall or kicked her up the stairs towards the bedroom, where he would continue to punish her for being a bad girl. He would force her into a corner and stand over her, spouting threats (she never knew if they were empty or if he fully intended to do the things he promised), and flailing his arms as though he were about to hit her again. She never knew what to do during those moments. Her mind told her to kick him in the balls as hard as humanly possible and run for dear life. Go to the kitchen, pick up a knife, get some money and her car keys, and leave the house. But that thought was always dissolved by the realization that if she ran, he could catch her. And when he did, that would be all she wrote. He would probably beat her to death and leave her body lying around on the lawn so that the neighbors could see how she died in disgrace. She knew that wasn't a rational thought, but she believed something similar to that would happen for sure. She knew that as well as she knew her own name.

So, more often than not, she cowered in the corner, the very same one she was crouching in then, and waited.

He was abusive. Both physically and mentally. She never knew which one she was going to get. If he had been out drinking, which he did often, she would get physically abused. He would come home frustrated about some game on television that he made a sucker's bet on with some drunk at the bar and take it out on her. He would smack her around a little, to make sure she knew her place, and then he would demand that she take off her clothes so that he could fuck her. It only lasted about two minutes from start to finish. He would push his way inside her, painfully splaying her legs and laying all of his weight on her stomach. He was oblivious to the shriek that escaped her as the friction of his erect penis rubbing against the flesh of her dry vagina chafed her, or the tears rolling down her cheeks from the degradation. He'd hump her maybe ten times, and then pass out on top of her, blowing his sour-sweet smelling breath in her face: a combination of beer, vodka, and cigarettes.

She would lie still for a couple of minutes to make sure that he was completely knocked out and then push his body off her in disgust and dissatisfaction. Sometimes she would satisfy herself after his accost. Sometimes the idea of having him inside her aroused her senses. Sometimes. Most times it just made her feel like her stomach was welling with a greasy film and she wanted to throw up.

After he was finished doing his business and he lay next to her, knocked out by the booze and the exerted energy, she would lie there in the dark, staring up at the ceiling and cry. Patty felt used, embarrassed, ashamed. She wanted to crawl into her own little shell and never come out. She hated him for it. For everything. But when he woke up the next morning, everything was peachy and rosy, and he acted like nothing had happened. No, it was more like he acted as if maybe he did something he shouldn't have, and that if he was extra nice and extra kind to her, she would forget about the whole thing. He either ignored the situation and made sure to stay out of her way, or he smothered her with flowers and dresses and shoes on some impromptu shopping spree. She saw right through it but didn't say anything. She kept thinking that maybe he really was sorry and that she was being unfairly judgmental of his actions. She would berate herself for not believing in him and not being a loyal wife who never contested anything her husband told her. She would guilt herself into thinking that somehow, she *deserved* that kind of treatment, and that when he was nice to her, he was showing her unbelievable mercy. Mercy that she didn't deserve from him.

Her father had been that way with her mother. She remembered hearing him shout and break things. Most of all, she remembered her mother's helplessness. Her father would come into the house in a rage most nights, stemming from something that happened at work, or at the track, or anything that rubbed him the wrong way. She could tell from the moment he closed the car door whether he was in a bad mood. He would storm into the house, calling for her mother. She would come out looking innocent, looking afraid. He wouldn't always hit her, no. What he would do instead was probably more damaging. He would slap her with insults about the tidiness (or lack of) of the house, about the laundry, about her appearance, about dinner, about the sun, about the moon, about the air. He would say anything he could think of to belittle her mother. He would reduce her to tears, but she would not, could not, leave the room. She would not cover her face. She would not respond. She was like a caged prisoner that was bound and gagged and forced to hear the lecture from a warden or a prison guard. It was difficult to see her mother looking frightened to death but not moving from the line of fire. To see her father, with his huge, broad shoulders hulking over her like she was a small child, terrified her to the core of her being and affected her throughout her life. She felt defenseless. There were so many times that she wanted to go to her mother. She wanted so desperately to help her get away from her father's fury, but she couldn't do anything. She was caught up in his trance as well.

Her mother died when Patty was fourteen years old. Her body (her shell) still walks around and talks to the people she comes in contact with. It still dances at parties, and drinks with the girls on Ladies Night Out. It still does all those things, but without a soul; without the essence of *her*. Her mother's soul died a long time ago at the hands of her father. The day her mother died pops into Patty's mind from time to time. It comes to her when she is frightened; when she thinks she is in trouble.

Patty's father came home one day after work. He was annoyed; she could tell that by the way he slammed the front door shut. Her mother walked slowly out of the kitchen and timidly said hello. She went to take his coat and hang it up for him, but he cringed away from her. She asked what was wrong, and he slapped her so violently that her body was thrown into the china cabinet...and it came tumbling down. The crash was deafening. It reverberated through the house.

But what was worse was the shriek her mother made when she was thrown. It was a high-pitched yelp, almost like a wounded animal's cry. Patty wanted to go to her. God, how she wanted to run to her mother and pick her up and take her to safety. The next-door neighbor's house, or even the corner store, would do. Anything to get away from her father. But she was too afraid to move.

He seldom hit. He liked to cut with his words too much to diminish the intensity and sting with physical force. He used to always tell her that a person who settles matters with his hands is not a man but is an animal. He said that a person who could handle himself or herself with their mind was far superior and would be the one who would evolve. He rarely abandoned that thought process. But when he did, he had good reason, at least in his mind. And there was hell to pay when he lost his temper. You'd better believe that. If he struck you with his hand, something must be seriously wrong. And there was no running from it, and no stopping it. It was going to happen one way or the other.

She hated to see her mother holding herself in the fetal position amidst the broken glass and china that was given to them for their wedding. She knew that the mess would prompt another beating later, before the bruises she was about to get could heal. Her mother would offer a meek apology for something or another, usually whatever she thought he wanted to hear, but it never worked. Nothing ever stopped him when he was like this. Nothing.

Her mother sat up to face him as he demanded. She was frozen. Her face was full of fear and distress. Her eyes called out for him to stop, to look at her and feel the love he felt when he asked her to be his wife. As he hulked over her and his ominous shadow crossed her face, something changed.

Her eyes, that had always begged forgiveness, now pleaded with him to get on with it. To end it all for her in one fell swoop. To shit or get off the pot. And, in a way, he did.

Her father stood over her shaking mother, who looked as if she were melting under his hot glare. She was so afraid to move. She waited, as she always did, for the next blow. It came. He hit her squarely on the side of her head, just under her temple. She fell sideways into the broken glass, cutting her right arm and leg. She yelled out in pain and begged him to stop.

Go ahead! Finish it, you bastard!

And he did. He stopped hitting her. He picked her up and carried her out of the glass. He dropped her heavily on the stairs and began screaming at her. He told her how much of a slut she was and how unfaithful she would be if he closed his eyes for just one minute. She asked him what he was talking about, and he threatened her with his open hand.

"Shut up, or I swear I'll hit you so hard you'll wish you were never born," he yelled. She lowered her eyes and began to weep.

"You'd better stop all that crying. What kind of woman lets her man see her cry? A weak one, right? Well, I guess that's just what you are, isn't it? A weak, needy woman. I don't know why I married you. You aren't worth the ring you wear on your hand. The ring you and your stupid friends coo over. You ain't worth shit."

He paced in front of the stairs Patty's mother lay upon, broken and bloodied. Anger welled up from his diaphragm as he continued.

"You are nothing but a whore. I thought you might be the trophy wife I had been searching for. The one who would look pretty yet say nothing. You certainly haven't turned out the way I had hoped you would. You are neither pretty nor obedient. Instead, you're wrinkled. Old, worn, and sassy. Just my luck.

"I have never wanted you, not even when you were young. You repulse me sexually. I wanted a woman who would do her duty and take care of my kids. But you wanted the job, and I let you do it. Why not? It's not like you could ever make more money than I do or ever accomplish more. I figured you had to be good for something in your worthless existence. But I was wrong. No, the only thing you are good at is flaunting what little you do have to my colleagues and bringing shame to my good name. How dare you?"

Confused and afraid, she said, "What are you talking about? I have no idea what you mean. I have never flirted with anyone; you must know that."

"I don't know much when it comes to you, my dear. Sometimes I wonder if I should have my head examined for even continuing this farce of a relationship with you. The only reason I am still here is because it looks better in my profession to be a married man. Even if I can't stand the sight of my wife."

Her eyes gave way to her tears. She couldn't take the abuse anymore, and it was breaking her down. She tried to hold in her tears, to hold in her emotions. She had been trying to learn to do that ever since he started coming home in these rages. But it never worked. She always ended up sobbing and shaking. She was sure she'd be able to take another smack for it, but she couldn't stop.

"Go on. Cry. That's all you seem to do well, anyway. You and your family are just a bunch of paupers. All of you walk around with your hands out, looking to get some spare change from a person who works hard for every dime. No, you may not be exactly like them, but the apple sure doesn't fall far from the tree, does it? All you ever want to do is whine about your job and the inequalities of men and women. What makes you think you should be equal? What makes you think that you have enough smarts, enough where-with-all, enough gumption, enough common sense to stand toe to toe with a man? Huh? Whoever told you that?"

He changed the subject often when he got angry enough. It was almost as if his mind was so full of hatred, he couldn't decide what he wanted to lash out about next. He liked to badger her on a variety of subjects so he could make sure he beat her self-esteem down to nothing. Sitting on the stairs, her face drenched with sweat; she didn't have much self-esteem to attack.

Her mother wanted to shout back, to retaliate, to clear herself, but she felt mute. And maybe that was a good thing. When he was like this—so headstrong and stubborn, so irate —you never knew exactly what he was capable of doing. She sat in silence, looking up at the man that she had married for better or for worse.

"Whoever told you that was lying, I will say that much. Get in the kitchen and cook my dinner, you worthless whore. And while you're at it, clean up this pigsty we try to call a house. You and that little bitch don't do anything in this house but eat the food I buy and sit around. Worthless. You were worthless when I got you, and you're teaching her how to be worthless as well."

From her hiding place in the hall, Patty saw her mother's light diminishing. She didn't know what half the stuff her father said meant, but she could tell by the look on her moth-er's face that he said something damaging. Her mother looked like a wilted flower on its last legs of life as she walked into the kitchen to find something to use to clean the mess up. The light that had always shone in her eyes, even when he was being abusive to her, flickered out that day, never to resurface. Not even after his death. Patty hated her father for breaking her mother spiritually and mentally. The woman that lived on was nothing like her mother. Nothing like the woman who had a positive outlook on life, who loved her unconditionally. What was left was a woman who barely knew where she was. A woman who didn't voice her feelings or her thoughts. A woman who cringed at the sound of a loud voice. She always blamed her father for the disintegration of her mother. He took her life in the blink of an instant, in the slice of a word.

Now, on the floor, in the corner of the bedroom she shared with her husband, with her knees pulled tightly under her chin, she knew that her light was gone too. She knew that she would never love the smell of freshly cut grass or feel the warmth of spring sunshine on her skin the way she once had. She knew that all the happy moments she would have from then on would be clouded with despair and fear, as her mother's life was. She felt trapped. It was the same feeling she had when she hid in the closet while her parents fought. She was afraid to get out of the closet and venture down the hall to her bedroom. She was too afraid her father would see her and turn his anger in her direction. She didn't have the courage to stand up in front of her father and shout at him to stop it. She could always feel the words welling in her gut while she cowered in the darkness. She could always feel them gurgling in her throat, threatening to come out. But she stifled them because she was too afraid. Too afraid of him.

Her mother always told her to be quiet when Daddy

yells, and to make sure she stayed in her room when Mommy and Daddy were talking loudly. She said that Daddy had a bad temper, and he might get mad that she was around. She said something like eavesdropping, and something about a child's place and some other catchy phrase that would pacify her for the time being. They never really worked. She just did what her mother told her to do because there was no other recourse. Disobeying Mommy when it pertained to Daddy could result in a whole lot of trouble that she didn't want. She was scared to death at the idea that her father could be angry at her. That meant he would shout at her the way he shouted at Mommy...or worse. She felt like she would melt right into the floor if he looked at her with his black, menacing eyes. She was afraid. Then and now. She shivered as she heard footsteps coming up the stairs.

He'll kill me if he finds out

The days grow colder and colder now. When she looks out of their bedroom window, she sees nothing but gray in the bright sunlight. There's nothing but gray inside as well. She hears angry voices shouting incoherently, as though they are trapped in the depths of her mind. Except one. There is one voice looming just under the surface, with horrifying clarity. Whispering cunningly, coaxing her to do unspeakable things.

She wrung her hands as she listened to the footsteps ascend. The car had pulled up just as she spilled the juice. It ran across the countertop and dripped onto the floor. She heard the garage door opening, creaking, signaling his arrival. The gentle hum of the motor cut off, and the car door slammed shut. Frantically, she reached for a paper towel to sop up the mess that started pooling on the floor. Bright red trickles fell relentlessly on the paper towel, saturating it. The garage door slammed shut, and she heard the paced footsteps rhythmically approaching the basement door, as if in slow motion. Instinctively, she ran upstairs, trying to hide herself.

He'll kill me if he finds out

Then she saw his eyes. Big and horribly bloodshot, as if someone had poured red dye into them. He saw the mess. He was not happy. Not happy at all.

Then there was nothing. The house was silent except for the scratching sound of the tree branches grazing the window. There were no footsteps climbing the stairs and no irascible eyes threatening her. She was alone, cowering in the corner of the bedroom she shared with her husband. Her gentle, hardworking husband, who was on a business trip in Florida.

Is he?

(you ungrateful bitch)

He had been gone for three days

Is the trip really business, or pleasure?

(fucking bitch)

And she was supposed to be packed and ready to go when he got back. They were going to the beach for a week, and he wanted to get on the road as soon as possible.

I'm leaving him.

(Do it)

She got up hesitantly, wondering if her mind was playing tricks on her. She couldn't tell if it was just trying to make her think the coast was clear when he was really waiting around the corner to pounce on her. She looked over at the packed bags on the floor. She had packed them herself, not five hours earlier. Still, she wasn't sure why she had done it, nor where she was going.

She peered around the door and saw nothing. Just an open hallway. She was alone. Alone except for that terrible whispering that echoed in her head.

She walked into the hallway feeling confused, but grateful that she had been mistaken. She turned to look at the grandfather clock in the foyer downstairs. It was almost 4:30 p.m. He would be gone for another day or so on a business trip. True to form, he would probably come home cranky. He was loud and belligerent when he was cranky.

Wouldn't he?

She decided that she wasn't going to stick around for it this time. She was going to leave. She was going to get up her nerve and leave him, like she had been telling herself to do for months (*had she?*) ...but just for a little while. She couldn't leave him altogether, like the voice in her head kept telling her to do. She wasn't ready to start a life without him. She wasn't ready to be alone.

She went back into the bedroom they shared and packed some of her things, forgetting that she had already packed clothes for the beach vacation. She walked right past the vacation bag, pulled out an overnight carryall, and threw a nightgown, shorts, underwear, and sandals in. She only wanted to scare him. She wanted to make him *think* that he was losing her forever. That way, he would do everything he could, to straighten up and try to get her back. At least, she hoped that would be his reaction.

As she packed, she thought about the good times they had, like when he picked her up from work one day with roses in one hand and concert tickets in the other. He was so handsome, so stunning. She couldn't help but be swept off her feet. His beautiful brown eyes always seemed to see right through her. He would smile at her innocently, shy almost, like he was unsure if he should be so forward, even now. They had been married for a while, but he still had a timidity about him that was intriguing and captivating. It was part of his charm. He rendered her defenseless when he complimented her on her dress and then lowered his head, as if he was too bashful to look her in the eyes. She missed the times when he would kiss her so gently she questioned if their lips were even touching. He used to caress her feet after a long day at work. He would whisper in her ear about how much he loved her. He supported her decision to stop working so that she could stay at home and start a family. And when Michelle came along, Troy treated her and the baby like they were his most prized possessions.

Michelle. Their bundle of joy. She was a gift that rejuvenated their relationship for a short time. That was until Patty realized that Troy cared more about the baby than he did about her. Michelle could do no wrong. She was precious, a gem. With him she was good: she smiled at him the first time, walked to him, said 'Dada' first. Daddy's little girl. For mommy, all she had was defiance, messes, vomit, and mischievousness. Didn't he hear that incessant crying in the middle of the night when she was an infant? Couldn't he see how she was warming up to him in an attempt to alienate her? Couldn't he see how manipulative she was? At two years old, that little girl knew exactly what she wanted and how to get it.

Something you used to know

(*ungrateful bitch*)

Patty thought about Michelle sleeping in her crib/bed combo, surrounded by plush teddy bears – presents from daddy. She shuddered despite herself.

Troy used to love her the way he loved Michelle...once. As tears welled in her eyes, she realized that those days had been gone for a long time. She wanted them back desperately. She just didn't know if those times could be again.

(Or if they had ever ended)

She went into the garage and loaded up the car. It was unseasonably cold for October—with the wind whipping around; it felt like it could have been 10 degrees below zero. She could see the leaves blowing around her driveway from the little window in the one-car garage door. It gave her a chill. She started the car to warm it up for the drive ahead. She wasn't exactly sure where she was going yet. She was having a mental tug of war between leaving him for good or only leaving for the night.

And there was something else too. Something she was missing.

Or forgetting.

Life with Troy had been bittersweet. The ups were magnificent, yet few and far between. The downs had been more prevalent and damaging. They didn't fight like normal couples do. They could never figure out how to have an argument, agree to disagree, and then end it. It just didn't work with them. Instead, they would yell and scream and rant and rave until he had enough. When he reached his saturation point, he would hit her, and she would be silent. From that point on, the ball was in his court. Whatever he said went, and nothing else could carry any weight. Depending on how angry he got, he would hit her several times, beckoning for her to tell him if she understood the rules of the house. His rules. She would say yes time and time again, but he would still beat her until he got tired. Then he would storm out of the house and do God knows what for a couple of hours. They fought like that a lot.

She closed the trunk and leaned against the car. The low, steady hum of the engine was soothing, and it lulled her into a daydream. She thought back to when they were in Jamaica, walking along the beach, him in shorts, her in a short sundress. Looking out at the turquoise water and enjoying their love. They were so happy then. It was their first trip together, and they had been planning it for months. They were staying in a rinky-dink hotel, but it didn't matter to them. They just wanted some time to get away, to relax, and to learn more about each other. They made love for the first time on a secluded beach at midnight. They held each other under the stars and dreamt of their life together. It was like a fairytale. One that didn't come true. She wiped the tears from her eyes and opened the car door.

She sat in her car, unable to move for a while. She felt weak with despair and simple with love. The sun was going down, and a branch from a willow tree cast a shadow on the dashboard on the passenger side of the car. It was in the shape of an index finger. It pointed directly at her, either shaming her for staying so long, or shaming her for leaving.

(*Or shaming you for Michelle*)

"Shut up," she screamed aloud, covering her ears with her hands and rapidly shaking her head back and forth. She didn't know which one was true. All she knew was that she felt helpless and lost. She didn't know where to turn.

How long had she been sitting in the car, she wondered? A minute? An hour? She guessed it had been even longer than that. It had been bright and sunny when she ventured into the garage, and now night was threatening its entrance. In the gray light of her car, she opened her diary and scribbled in it. There wasn't much to say, really. She expressed her indecisiveness daily to the pastel pages within that book. It was her only outlet. She couldn't yell back at her husband for fear of being beaten, so she used the diary as a sounding board. She couldn't express her feelings (love? hate?) to

Michelle aloud anymore. She choked on the words. So, she wrote them all down. The entries were usually very short and jagged. Her thoughts were rarely in eloquently phrased sentences. This time, the last time, was no different.

As the smell of exhaust filled the air thickly, she cried into her hands. She couldn't make herself move. She felt like she had nowhere to go and that she was worthless. The big family that she had when she was young was gone. They had died off or distanced themselves. Seeing each other only rekindled the memories and the rumors, so no one made an effort anymore. The last time she saw her family was when they gathered together for her Aunt Clairese's funeral. She was in her Aunt Clairese's house, trying to remain contained, when she saw the thing that unraveled her. She and her aunt had never been close. They had never played together, or talked silly talk, or even taken walks in the park. All they had ever done was see each other at family functions or funerals. They would hug, talk for five minutes, and that would be all. There wasn't a tight connection between the two of them. But when she stood in Aunt Clairese's living room and saw an old picture of herself sitting on the very top of the mantel, dusted and clean, she buckled. The sofa caught her fall. She had never, not in a million years, thought that her aunt cared enough about her to think of her outside of when they saw each other at family gatherings. She thought that her Aunt regarded her as just 'one of those relatives' that you could take or leave. She never thought that her aunt might actually care about her, that she might actually love her. Years of guilt engulfed her at the moment.

In the years after Aunt Clairese's death, the family broke apart. It wasn't a surprise. There was always a storm brewing underneath the facade of happy faces and family love. She hadn't seen her cousins in years, probably since the funeral. There was nothing to say, really. Whatever happened before they were born was too great to overcome, it seemed. So, everyone dropped the ball. They dropped the ball and kicked it in the corner.

All the friends she had a couple of years ago were gone. They moved on with their lives and rarely kept in contact. She missed the nights when she would go out drinking with the girls and checking out guys. They used to sit around and talk about nothing, but that was OK because it passed the time. She used to go shopping with Troy's sister Cheryl, and they would stay out all day not buying a thing. That all ended when Troy told her that he didn't like Cheryl and Patty spending so much time together. He said that he never really liked Cheryl and didn't want her to be a negative influence on Patty. His own sister! She did what he wanted because she thought this was the man she would live with for the rest of her life. She did it for love.

That's what the voice told her to do.

Cheryl faded out of the picture without much of a fight. It wouldn't have mattered if she protested anyway; there was no changing the plan. If having Cheryl out of the picture would make Troy happy, then, by God, that's what she was going to do. She lost a lot of friends because of Troy. They either didn't want to be around her because all she ever did was talk about Troy, or Troy didn't want them around. She compromised her dignity to feed his ego. She geared her life toward making him happy and, in the process, forsaking her own happiness. She wasn't doing things for herself anymore. Everything was for Troy. She lost her road. She also lost herself.

The voice in her head told her so.

**

Troy Johnson came home around 2:30 p.m. the next day, dying for a real shower. Hotels never seemed to have the right water pressure, at least not the cut-rate establishments his company put him up in. He wanted food, a shower, and some lovin' from his wife. He missed her more on this trip than he ever had, even though he had only been gone for three days. He called her the night before, asking her to leave Michelle with his sister so he could get some uninterrupted R&R when he got home, but there was no answer. Knowing her, she was probably out gallivanting in the street with her friends. Although that seemed a little odd for her in the middle of the week. She usually waited until the weekend to hang out with them. He hated that. They had fought over it several times in the past couple of months, to no avail. Her argument was that she lived with Troy. He was her husband. She saw him all the time. Why shouldn't she want to spend time with her friends? She said it was a release to be out with them. A release from what? he wondered. He was never home anyway!

She called him selfish and a pansy, no less, for wanting to spend time with her. Is there something wrong with a man wanting to spend quality time with his wife on the weekend? Is there something wrong with a man who would rather spend all his time with his wife than with some sweaty men playing basketball or shouting over a game on television? He thought that was what women wanted. He thought they wanted a man who would work all week and devote his weekends to his woman. Not his lady. No, she wanted her man to work all week, bringing home the bacon for her to do whatever she wanted with, and to cook and clean on the weekends while she was out having fun and partying with her friends. Or maybe she would go gallivanting at the malls with her cousin Ann. There was always some function that the two of them had to buy a new dress for. Oh, and you can't just buy the dress. You had to buy the shoes, a handbag, maybe a scarf, and a new shade of lipstick. You had to coordinate things. It made no sense to him, but who was he to argue about what a woman needs?

Sometimes, she would give him a couple of hours on the weekend. All they ever did was make love, because there really wasn't enough time to do anything else. She always had somewhere to be, some show to see, some fire under her ass. She could never sit still long enough for Troy to think about planning a day for them. Before Michelle and after.

When Patty told him that she wanted to stop working to start having children, he fully supported her decision because he wanted children desperately. If she didn't want to work, she didn't have to. He made enough money to support them. She stopped working and started sitting around the house. Sulking. He didn't understand it. She didn't want to even talk about the prospect of having a family, let alone try to get pregnant. All she wanted to do was sulk around the house during the week and go out and party on the weekends. It wasn't like her. It wasn't like her at all.

He hated the way she was acting, but he loved her. When he was away on business, he missed her so much, even though she paid him no attention when he was at home. He had hoped that time would change her, make her into a wife who wanted to spend time with her husband. So far, no good. It was strange.

Ever since the wedding, she had been acting distant. She got worse after the baby. She was cold to all of her cousins, only talking to them when she wanted them. As a matter of fact, she was cold to them at the wedding, and none of them had come around or called more than three times in the couple of years since that day. Before the wedding, she had worked so hard to get close to her family. They had always been distant because of some old family circumstances, but Patty seemed determined to fix things. Not having any siblings and living thirty minutes away from the rest of her family, the relationship with her cousins resembled that of acquaintances rather than family. But she worked at it.

Just as she started to get close with the family, going out to the movies and having dinner parties with some regularity, she pulled away. It was right around when her Aunt Clairese died. She stopped going to family functions and stopped calling. When they would call, she wouldn't come to the phone. She kept her relationship with Troy's sister Cheryl, though, but that changed as well.

As soon as Patty and Troy started dating, she and Cheryl hit it off. They became inseparable. His mother used to joke that Troy had to marry Patty if he didn't want to be disowned by the family. They had the kind of relationship that was so easy; it was almost like they were the same person. He envied that. Patty never let him in the way that she let Cheryl in. But then, all of that changed.

Patty started calling the shots. Cheryl tried to get together with her, but Patty always seemed to have something more important to do. Patty only saw Cheryl when Patty wanted to. Nothing more. Just like that. Troy tried to get them all together, her family and his, for a mid-winter party, but she didn't want to. She would tell him that she wanted to move on and live her life away from 'those people'. He didn't push it, but he wondered sometimes about the reason for her sudden change. They were all on their way to becoming close; to becoming a family, the way she always wanted them to be.

She was worse with Michelle. Patty finally got pregnant and gave birth to Michelle a month before their second anniversary. Michelle was a good little girl. She rarely cried and always had a smile for everyone, yet Patty disliked her. At first, Troy thought it was post-natal depression, but it was more than that. She said Michelle embodied everything good that was in her; that Michelle had taken it out of her. She wasn't mean to Michelle, really; she was a good mother. But there was always something just beneath the surface, something unrecognizable.

He opened the garage with the remote and got ready to pull in. Her car was still there. A smile grew wide across his face. *Maybe she cleared her day so that she could spend it with me,* he thought to himself, and grinned like a schoolboy with his first crush. Maybe they could grab a bite to eat, or catch a movie, he thought to himself. At the very least, maybe he could talk her into taking a hot shower with him. He wanted to be with her, to make her see that he really did care about her. She had been going off on these tangents recently about how she didn't think he loved her, or that she didn't think she was good enough for him. Almost as soon as they were married, she started having these questions about his love and their compatibility. She had never talked like that before. He had been trying to talk her out of her confusion, but it was beginning to wear on him. He had been considering getting her to see someone about her thoughts of inadequacy. He even told her that he would go too, but it didn't help. She adopted the notion that he thought she was crazy. He left it alone. He didn't want to aggravate the situation any further. He just kept showering her with love, hoping that she would snap out of it in time.

He closed the garage door, parked his car in the driveway, and hopped out of the car. The crisp air blew open his coat as he bopped to the front door, happily anticipating seeing his wife standing in the doorway in a beautiful negligee. He opened the door slowly. When he saw that she wasn't there, he thought maybe she was taking a nap. He tried to sneak around the house, hoping that he would surprise her. He wanted to see her eyes light up. He went through the house, up into the bedrooms, into the bathroom, the kitchen, the game room, and he even looked in the backyard, but he didn't see her. Discouraged, he went back into the kitchen to see if there was a note. That was their system. They left notes on the kitchen counter if they had taken a walk or were over at the neighbor's house. He didn't know why he hadn't thought to look there first. He had been so excited to see her that he just forgot about that possibility.

Then he heard Michelle crying.

Troy was paralyzed. 'The baby is crying upstairs,' he thought. 'Where is Patty?'

His eyes fell upon the door that leads to the garage, and his spine went cold. Unsure of why he felt sudden terror, he approached the door slowly. Michelle's crying had not subsided, but he barely heard it anymore.

When he opened the garage door, he was greeted by the faint smell of exhaust. The car was on, and he saw his wife sitting in the driver's seat. His first thought was that he had just caught her, but when he got closer, he saw that he was too late. He opened the car door and was greeted by a pungent rotting smell. His stomach gurgled in revulsion, and he dropped to his knees. He looked up at his wife through the fogged glass of the driver's side car door. Her lips were bluish black, and her skin was chalky. Her eyes were open and swollen. She had faint tracks on her face that looked like the stains from tears. Open on the seat next to her was the diary that she had just purchased the day that he left for his business trip. She told Troy when she kissed him goodbye at the front door three days ago that she wanted to keep a journal for him to read so that he would know how much she loved him. She told him that she would write in it every time she thought of him. She assured him that all the pages in the book would be filled before a week was out. She was right about that. Some of the pages were dog-eared, and writing covered every line; even the margins had notes in them. He wondered if the words on the page would satisfy his questions in the days to come or just add to his confusion.

She bought the diary during one of her more sensitive times. She got into a sappy mood every so often. For Troy, they were enough to balance out the sour times when she was negative and confrontational. But as he looked into her blank eyes, he realized that there would never be another sappy time for her. Or him.

POLICE FILE #003.9879
EVIDENCE TYPE: Letter, handwritten
HISTORY: N/A
Tuesday, May 19, 1970

Dear Troy,

I'm trying desperately to say what I really mean this time. I don't want any intrusion of that voice that has been terrorizing me and tormenting our relationship for so long. I don't want it to sprout up and distort my feelings again. Not this time.

I can't control it anymore, baby. I keep thinking that you are coming to get me, coming to punish me for something, when I know in my heart that you're not. You've never been that kind of man. I was confused about that for a long time, but now I finally know the truth. You are a despicable person, and I wish you'd rot in hell, you bastard. You won't get the chance to fuck with me again; I'll see to that. That was my father, not you. He was the one who came after Mom, not me. At least, I think that's what happened. I can't be sure now. Everything is so screwed up in my head.

Michelle too. I thought she was trying to ruin me, to take everything from me. To eat me from inside, to play with my intestines like they were jump ropes. But I know now that she only wanted to be loved.

Do you play now, Michelle?

I know now that there is something living within me—something awful—that fills me with these horrible thoughts. I can hear the voice in my head. It whispers to me when I look in the mirror or when I'm in the shower. It whispers so low sometimes I don't think I hear it. It just wants to make sure it has my full attention. It wants to make sure that I am listening to what it says. It seems like it talks to me all the time now. I know you think that sounds crazy. I would too if I were in your shoes. But it really is happening to me, Troy. It's a part of me; I know that now. I don't know what triggered it or why it's here, but it is, and it's been here for a long time. You have been such an unbearable entity in my life that I've got to end it to fully be detached from you, you motherfucker.

This thing, this voice, tells me that you hate me and that you are going to leave me. I sit all day wanting you to come home from work so that I can be with you, but then I am frightened to death at the sight of you. I'm afraid to go out because I see scars and bruises on my face from where you've hit me, and I don't want anyone else to see them. They are always fresh. But you couldn't have done those things to me. I know it. I know it's true on one side of my head—the sane side. But the other side, this dark and ominous side, tells me otherwise.

I beat myself the other day. I only caught a glimpse of it in the mirror. Only it didn't look like me at all. My face was distorted in pain and fear, distended like an egg. It was the most horrible sight I'd ever seen. And then, just like that, I didn't see anything anymore. It wasn't like I blacked out or anything...I just didn't see what I was doing to myself. It's like I imagined that you were the one doing it...and it became real to me. And the scary part about it was that I liked it. I think it—the voice—wanted me to see it. I think it wants me to go crazy, because then it will have won, and it can have me for as long as it wants. It can make me do horrible things without having to deal with the sane side putting up resistance. I think it wants me to hurt Michelle. Well, that's not going to happen. I won't let it happen. I'll kill her before it gets its hands on her.

I have to do this, Troy. For all of us. You deserve to have a happy life with someone who can love you the way you need to be loved. You shouldn't have to deal with a person who can't take hold of her fucking whorish self long enough to love you like a real man should be fucked. I shouldn't show the pink of my brain matter, just like you shouldn't see the pink of my pussy. You've contaminated me enough, haven't you? And to think, all you want is more, more, more. Maybe you'll like what you see when you look in the mirror at your blood-streaked face. The afterlife has a world of things waiting for us. There are jump ropes for Michelle and bitches for you. But what is there for me?

Michelle needs a mother who can care for her the way she needs to be cared for, the ungrateful bitch. I can hear her mewling now; the incessant timbre is enough to drive me mad.

I feel like I'm losing control of it now, so I think

it's time. Fuck you, Troy. I love you and Michelle very much.

Patty

INTERVIEW (ONSITE): NA

\/\\\/\/\\\/

CLARITY OF THOUGHT

HE INCHED CLOSER, fingers reaching like tentacles to graze skin. He didn't know whose skin he might touch, and it didn't matter; he simply needed connection. He'd given of himself before, swore he would never do it again, but here was, wanting, needing, actively seeking... someone.

Anyone.

The door obliged, but that wasn't what he wanted. Stuck half in and half out of the garage as he had been for what could've been hours as easily as seconds, he found the interior of the car suffocating, as if the doors, the headliner with its yellowed light cover and puckered roof, the very upholstery on the seats inched closer with his every breath, closer like a boa constrictor to tighten around him. Closer, closer, ever closer. Something was back there, behind the car. Something he couldn't see.

But it could see him.

He'd walked down the steps in the garage and over to the driver's side door the same way he did every day. It was one of those things people did on autopilot, completing tasks while their minds were otherwise occupied with bills, presentations, dinner plans, everyday worries. He was alone in the garage, which made sense. He lived by himself, and the space was his and his alone, connected to the three-level townhome that he was still furnishing after two years. Being alone never bothered him because he could change that when he wanted to, could go outside and join the throng of people jogging, walking the sidewalks, shopping in big box stores. He could have a conversation with someone at the gas pump, in the supermarket, at the fast-food place if he wanted to use his voice. He could take himself off mute in meetings and actually contribute to the conversation if he really needed to take part. He could do any of those things in his own time, so alone was good, alone was comfortable, alone was what he wanted it to be, when he wanted it to be. Alone never crossed anyone's mind until it needed to, until being so was dangerous. That day was no different.

He stopped in the garage and reached for the car door, ready to get into the car. He had errands to run, solitary ones where he didn't have to speak with anyone at all if he didn't want to. Drop mail in the slot. Top off the air in his tires. Withdraw money from the ATM. He was plotting his route absently as he got in the car, not thinking about the movements actively as much as his body propelled him toward an end, activating to move him toward a path. The buzz beneath his fingers as he touched the door handle didn't register until after he got in the car and started it up, the remnant of the unexpected tingle lingering there to numb his fingers as they curled around the scalloped steering wheel. He looked at his hand, flexed the fingers under his gaze, and placed it back on the steering wheel as the sound of the car engine filled his ears. He pressed the button on the remote to open the garage door, couldn't feel the plastic beneath his fingers. He brought his hand back to the steering wheel. He started the ignition. His hand still felt wrong, false, like rubber, so he took it off the steering wheel again to slap it against his thigh. False, false, like a prosthetic.

Like it was someone else's.

The garage door opening was loud on the track.

He leaned toward his hand, turning his wrist so that he could examine the fingers closely, and that's when it happened. The beep of a vehicle in reverse; the chime of an alert when something is detected in the sensor, when something is in the car's path rang in the cabin. A beep that shouldn't be because he had not yet put the car in reverse.

The camera flickered to life as he looked, finding himself eye to eye with the display since he'd bent so low to examine his numb fingers, and he saw nothing that would indicate a reason for concern. The garbage can hadn't been left in front of the garage door where he could hit it this time, nor had a package been left there. He always checked for that now; he'd crushed a gift from his mother years before, a box full of housewarming bits and bobs all mutilated by the tread of his tires, and then there was the box filled with things that spoke of love that he'd all but annihilated under the car's weight, but there was nothing there this time. Nothing there. Nothing at all, until the sensor on the left side of the car began to glow, began to pulse, began to shriek.

He reached for the door with his numb hand, numb like gums injected with Novocain, he reached for it but didn't want it, didn't want it at all, because it couldn't save him. He would never be able to use it, to scramble to the other side of the car and open it so he could fall out onto the garage floor only to rise to his feet at a run; he'd never be fast enough for that. The sensor positively howled now, long wailing notes like ill-planned chords on a theremin, like the car was begging for help, so he knew that to reach for the door was futile. But flesh would have sufficed. Flesh would have helped him to make sense of the moment, to ground himself in the inevitability of it, and to find and give comfort. Living skin would have provided warmth, solace, and understanding; would have opened him to emotions he might not normally feel; the gooseflesh beneath his fingertips a conduit to an emotional awareness he had never known before. Sex in the senses, appreciated in the final seconds, because the car was wailing, it was mewling, crying like a mother over a child whose first and last breaths were taken within her arms, crying in despair and fear and loss like an animal in a trap.

Crying its warning about the thing he couldn't see.

The thing that inched closer and closer.

He locked his doors, slapping at the switch wildly, hoping for purchase, but he heard them disengage as soon as they had slid home. Beads of sweat sprang onto his brow, and he wiped at it with his numb, useless hand. His cry joined that of the sensor, its high-pitched beep seeming to adjust to form perfect harmony with his own. He reached again, across the passenger seat and into the void to touch, to feel, to be made whole for the last time, his mind begging for familiar skin, for commiseration, for flesh of any kind however cold, taut, or gelatinous. But there was only the door. The light streamed in to illuminate it, to wash it with bright sunlight he hadn't noticed before, so bright he would have had to shield his eyes to look through its rays to see the door clearly. Bright light calling him back, to, away, toward. But he couldn't look; he was too afraid to look away from the display, from the benign street shown behind him, cookie-cutter homes with only the colors of the shutters to differentiate them. He was too afraid to look away from the pulsating dot on the screen.

He braced himself for his fingers to meet the door once again, the plastic arm the last thing he'd find, warmed now by the light of the sun to trick him into thinking it was living flesh, flesh that would be impossible to occupy that space because nobody was supposed to be there. Dimensions had taken him far away from those who cared enough to send him boxes to be crushed under cars, and he occupied his space alone, alone, entirely alone.

So, he reached.

And he reached.

\\/\\\\|/\\\\|/

ILL-GOTTEN

It was hot and musty in the club even before the show got started. The air was thick, almost like you could see it hanging in front of you like wool, and Will had to stop himself from reaching out to touch it. He was surprised they would even let that many people in the place – had to be some kind of violation to have wall-to-wall standing room only events in the old, single stage bar, but it happened every week and nobody said anything. They would when the floor caved in. There'd be a whole lot of shit to say when that happened.

Will didn't intend to be there for that, even if Mack indulged him a little, let him have more time before they had to run.

But Will knew better.

Michelle, Renee, and Tip were nearby; Will had told them to stay close, kept reminding them about it like they were little kids on a playdate, and he was the weary parent acquiescing to a detour in the park. That's kind of how he felt, truth be told. He liked them all right; there wasn't anything wrong with them, unless you wanted to call Tip out on his wigger shit, pull his hat off and let the lights hit that blond crown. There was money in his low-hanging jeans, trust fund money that he didn't want the others to know about, but Will did. Will knew everything about him and the girls – he had known everything about every single one of them. Mack made sure he did, in case he needed to make something happen.

Keep that in your back pocket, he'd said. Old gangster shit. Will's back pocket was full of all kinds of things now.

Did they even say wigger anymore or was that from another life, another jump, some other blood stuck between him and Mack, or beyond, one that left behind remnants of shit that wouldn't mean anything to anyone that came after? Will didn't know and didn't have time to figure it out. Something big was coming if he could make the cards bump. The last run was a set up for him. Will had to make it count.

The beat was manufactured, nothing but muffled bass and what sounded like whispering, nothing like the music with live instruments that his grandfather used to play around the house. Will thought the 80s were bad... watered down, Jheri-curled whining that it was, and the 90s with passable slow music poisoned by sex-fueled lyrics, but this? This was on another level. He wished Mack hadn't come to him in his dreams, hadn't demanded his service, hadn't bothered with him at all. He didn't even know how to use the wormhole he had reached through to fuck with Will – Mack only knew that he *could* do it, so he did. Mack would keep on doing it until he got what he wanted and though Will tried his best not to think about how many people get tapped for the job if he couldn't deliver – how many had already tried and failed – he couldn't stop his mind from going there, drawn to the thought like a beacon. Their eyes. Something inside him wanted to count their eyes, but Will shook the thought away. No more. Will was determined to make it stop... that night.

Michelle and Tip were dancing close, sparks flying between them, and Will wondered why they didn't just fuck already – leave the dancefloor and do the deed. They might not have the chance to after this – none of the others who had taken the ride with him ever got the chance to do anything but spill their blood on the asphalt and die. Will didn't have any reason to believe it would be any different for them either, and in the end, that didn't really matter. He only hoped that Mack knew why it had to be done and that he was right about it. After seeing what happened to the ones who had tried before, Will knew he only had one shot – there would be no time to even take a breath after meeting the breach.

He was in his head.

Will was stuck in his head, and he knew he shouldn't be. Worrying about what had happened or not happened was a mistake. It would make him slow, sluggish, nostalgic for something that was never his to mourn. But, still, he had seen all their faces, ignorance and youthful optimism coloring their expressions the way it should color his, but would not... not ever again.

Will had seen their faces as flesh separated from muscle, skulls gleaming in the cold fluorescent light under an inky sky.

He had seen them... as he slept. He had watched as their mouths gaped, wishing them away, their swift passage his only desire. And though he didn't want to, he remembered.

He remembered them all.

When the man bumped into him near the bar, bodies packed so tight he couldn't help but do so, Will didn't hear what he said in response, and that was good. The response the man would have uttered would have helped Will figure out what decade he was in at the very least, maybe even the actual year, but knowing how to respond might be a challenge. A misstep would make him stand out. Overthinking would bring on that misstep, so he didn't. He didn't look at the man either, for fear that he might stare. Will couldn't afford that, didn't have time for the problem that might come from it. Instead, he reminded himself that he belonged there, in that time and place. It was his, regardless of what Mack had shown him. He was himself, and he was right where he was supposed to be.

Except that he couldn't be sure anymore, not when he could find an onyx pinky ring next to an afro pick on the nightstand where his cell phone charged. No, he couldn't be sure of anything anymore.

Biggie Smalls was asking for one more chance, but that didn't mean anything; the greats play forever. KRS-One had just been booming through the speakers with a track from a decade before Biggie's hit; yeah, some shit is immortal. But Biggie coming through the speakers gave Will a starting point, one that made him feel even more confident that this time he could pull it off.

Because no one else had been able to do that yet.

If they had, what would he be doing now? Will knew it was foolish to think about that, to worry about what might have been, but he couldn't help it. Would he be across the country like he had planned when he thought he had some say in what came next? Would he have been traveling the world, maybe have gotten married and seen the sights with her? Would his mother still be alive if the dreams hadn't come... if Mack or one of the others had done what they set out to do and left him out of it? This was the question he hated most, because he knew the answer. Part of him wanted to kill Mack for it, even though he knew that was as ridiculous as threatening a corpse in a casket. But still, it's what he would do if it were possible. And who knows? None of what was going on – what had *been* going on since Mack had shown him everything – should be possible. So maybe, just maybe, there was a way to kill that motherfucker before Will sliced his own throat. Because that was what the other part of him wanted to do: kill himself, remove himself from the gameboard: lights out. It was only right that he do so after what he was planning to let happen to Michelle and Renee and Tip. He would think of his mother when he did it too, would make sure he conjured up her dying eyes to stare at him while he breathed his last breath. He'd hoped she knew it was for her, even though she would never have wanted it. But it was what was right, and he was a good boy, after all. If there was anyone watching, anyone who cared about penance in any real way, Will would be able to do that for her.

Like a fly on the wall, Will had been disturbed from a dreamless sleep and brought into a room that existed in a time long before his. He was made to listen as Mack and his partner talked about things Will didn't understand. Will recognized Mack from an old photo album – a cousin; his mother's grand-uncle's son or something like that. He had been wearing what could only be described as a zoot suit in the picture Will saw, pinstriped and replete with a chain dangling from hip to knee. The picture showed him standing with three other people – two women, one man – whose Will's mother did not know. They weren't written on the back in his grandmother's neat cursive either. 'Friends', she had labeled them simply, and that is how they would stay in perpetuity, at least in his family's records. The photo was dated 1955 – no month, no day. Will hadn't seen the picture a lot; it wasn't one that sat on their mantle, so he wasn't sure if the man in the room with Mack was one of the two in the picture as well, but that wasn't what was forefront in his mind when he came to grips with who he was seeing.

He knew immediately that it wasn't a dream. He also understood, with all clarity, that this was the fork in the road.

"I mean, the first Negro talkie was shot here," the other man said.

"The what?"

"The first Negro movie with sound... it was shot right here."

"*What?*"

Will's long-lost cousin looked irritated, and instantly he knew that sometimes the other man got on Mack's nerves talking about random shit. Mack sent the other man every signal he could to hurry things up. He looked at his watch, frowned over the time, pulled his eyes away to stare daggers at the other, then checked his watch again for good measure. When Mack spoke again, he was exasperated, beyond frustrated.

"What are you talking about, Carl?"

"Yeah," Carl said, stuffing his mouth with corn nuts, crunching them with his back teeth so loudly it made the bum in the corner stir. "Oscar Micheaux did it. Shot it right downtown."

Carl pointed toward the entrance they had used to get into the alley, and Will knew with all certainty that they had entered that way many times over many years. The entrance was in the direction of the George Washington Bridge, that connected New Jersey and New York through Fort Lee and Manhattan. Then Carl switched angles abruptly to point in the other direction.

"Or, no… I think it was that way. Wait… I'm screwed up," he said as he shifted his attention to the original direction he had pointed in again, a question on his lips.

"None of this shit would have been here then, so I'm all turned around, Mack, but it was here, that's for sure. Right here in Fort-"

"Nobody gives a shit about some old movie that was shot here!"

Will knew Mack didn't mean to yell as loud as he did – he could sense his cousin's thoughts. The idea of that tele-pathic connection was so disconcerting, it made Will dizzy. But it was real. Will knew that Mack hadn't meant to yell like that, not because he didn't want to hurt Carl's feelings, but because of the bum in the room. Mack didn't want to have to deal with another surprise. Will had the distinct impression that there had been many surprises along the way.

"It's history, Mack. It's important."

"Not to me, and it shouldn't be important to you… not if you know what's good for you."

He'd done it.

He'd threatened his best friend.

Will could feel the man's consternation, understanding context that he shouldn't. It had only taken 20 years to get to that point, and both men knew nothing good would come of it.

"It *better* mean something to *you*," Carl said as he stood to his full six feet, "if you know what's good for *you*."

Carl was imposing, and he knew it. Mack tried to glower back, but his heart wasn't in it. Carl knew that too.

"Carl...?" Mack said, unpuffing his chest, hoping that would be enough to cool things down. "What are you going on about? We need to get a move on – we don't have time to fool around with-"

"*The Exile* – that was the name of it," Carl continued as if he hadn't heard Mack talking, and while that made Mack angry, he knew there wasn't anything he could do about it. He'd made the mistake of trying to use his weight to force Carl into doing something once, and it was like running up against a brick wall. He wasn't interested in being repositioned like a child again, so he waited him out.

When Carl sat back down on an upended milk crate, Mack was relieved. Will knew all of this like he knew his own name.

"Made it back in 1931," Carl continued, the southern drawl of his people taking root in his pace, if not his pronunciation. "It's about a cowpoke who falls in love with a city girl, something like that. She's rich and wants to open a club or whatever they used to call it... a speakeasy, yeah. Anyway, they-"

"Carl!" Will saw Mack tense, as if he expected the interruption to earn him one on the chin, but it was a chance he thought he had to take.

"History is *important*, Mack," Carl said, his eyes trained on his friend in a way that made him look soulless.

Mack's jaw worked; his teeth were grinding into powder as they sawed their way down to the gum. But Carl kept on.

"It's the ignorant who can't see that, and they will always

be in the dark. As much as you come and go, you should care what goes on in between."

Mack's skin felt hot, and Will felt flushed too, especially when Carl looked away from him, ignoring the mounting anger on Mack's face to gaze thoughtfully at the high-rises peeking out from the mouth of the alley.

"She ain't mean us no harm," Carl said mournfully, looking at his calloused hands lying limp in his lap, "not at first. But we couldn't let well enough alone, could we? We just had to go, had to see. Once we caught a whiff of what smelled good, we had to have it."

"Carl," Mack started, but Carl kept talking.

"Ain't supposed to do folks like that. I knowed it, and you did too. But it called to us like a bitch in heat, ain't it? I couldn'ta said no even if I tried. Be careful, pap. Be careful what you ask for, 'cause them roots'll get you."

"Carl," Mack tried again, and this time the man looked at him with solemn eyes. "You's just tired, that's all. Just tell me where you put it and I'll get it back for us. We'll be livin' high on the hog uptown. Get us some dancin' girls to warm our beds. Come on, man, just tell me."

Carl's laugh came from deep in his chest and started slowly, bubbling up, building on itself as it rose to the surface. Mack didn't much like that – it made the hairs on his neck stand on end. Will could feel Mack's resolve cracking.

"What's so damn funny, man? Look," Mack said, shooting a glance around the room before lowering his voice, "we gotta get that shit before somebody else does, ok? It's *ours. We* did the work for it, not some, some bum who's gonna find it and run off."

Mack pointed at the man on the floor, but Carl did not look at him.

"It's ours, man. Let's get what's coming to us."

Carl's laughter roared in the dilapidated room, and a mix of emotions danced across Mack's face. Will could see that Mack was contemplating striking him; the tension in his body was as readable as words written on a page. But Carl didn't notice. He wheezed, though his chest ached, trying to take in enough air to speak. It was harder to do now; Carl's breath grew labored and shallow as he deteriorated before Mack's eyes.

"Oh, we'll get what's coming to us... no matter how long it takes, we'll get it." It hurt... Will could see that everything hurt the man now, even though he had appeared strong moments before.

"Yes!" Mack said animatedly, his furrowed brow releasing as Carl spoke the words, misreading the message and thinking his friend was coming around. "That's right, my man. We will get what's coming for us, that's for damn sure. Just tell me where you put it and I'll get it *for* us."

Carl nodded, still laughing. Mack was almost jumping up and down; his excitement was so complete.

"It's time."

"It is, man. It's long overdue, I'd say. But you know what, you're always right on time."

Carl stopped laughing abruptly and looked at the man he had called friend once upon a time. Disdain colored his features. His lips curled into a snarl before he spoke again.

"It's time to pay the piper, Mack."

Mack deflated as Will stared on incredulously. Mack didn't notice what was happening in front of him, didn't see what Carl was going through. Instead, he punched at the air in frustration, expending the anger and pent-up energy that had gathered in his joints as he coaxed Carl out. Had his friend grown senile waiting in that place? Was there really a screw loose like his mama thought there always had been? Mack had never wondered before, but the prospect was too hard to ignore now.

"... can't just go on like we don't have to. We owe, and they gonna collect."

Carl had been talking, but Mack hadn't been listening. He wasn't listening when he cut in either, not really. All he knew was that this – all of it – was bullshit.

"Are you calling me stupid, Carl? Huh?"

Mack's voice was loud, but he didn't care. Not even his mama called him stupid, and he wasn't going to stand there and take that kind of guff from someone who hadn't even finished the 6th grade.

"I may not know whether I'm coming or going most of the time, but that don't mean I'm stupid. Are you saying I don't have no sense-"

And then it hit him – Will could see understanding dawning on Mack's face. It was a terrifying sight.

"Christ, I *have* been stupid," Mack said, in awe. "Dumber than a doornail, in fact. 1931, you say," he whispered, and Will felt like he could see lights dancing in his eyes. "The year the bridge went up."

Carl nodded, and Will could tell that he was pleased with Mack for the first time in he didn't know how long. "I put it where the first Negro sound movie was made by the biggest Negro movie maker there had ever been, at least at that time. I'm sure you've seen bigger now. Me? I'll never get up from here, won't be here when you get back neither, and that's ok. Something that hard to have ain't for me no way, I guess."

Carl looked beyond Mack at the bum on the floor, and

Will followed his gaze. He almost screamed out loud when he saw the man's countenance in two places – animated in one and stone dead in the other. Will looked back at Carl quickly, feeling seen.

"That movie... the bridge... man, it's brilliant," Mack gushed. "How did you even *think* of that?"

Carl ignored Mack as he marveled over how intricate the plan had been, all while trying not to let the admission that he would never have figured it out on his own leave his lips. Instead, Carl mused like an old man sitting in a rocking chair on a porch before a setting sun. He nodded in the direction of the George Washington Bridge.

"That's the world's very first two-level suspension bridge right there, did you know that? Went up the same year Micheaux did his thing. To me, can't be one without the other." Carl kept talking, his eyes never leaving the bum's body in the corner, his own flesh where it fell. "Why'd I do that? Because history is important, Mack. It's everything."

Carl leaned in and for a second, Will wondered if he was about to slug Mack after all. But instead, he said, low so nobody could hear,

"Find Metropolitan Studios and you finds the money."

When Will had woken up in bed the next morning, he had questions. When did the dream take place? It couldn't have been 1931, because they were talking about that year as though it had been in the past. Not in 1955 like the date on the back of the picture – the man in the picture with Mack had been sporting a pompadour and there was not even the suggestion of one on Carl's head, though he might not have been in the picture at all – that was a possibility Will couldn't afford to forget. But something about Carl seemed more modern than that. Somehow, he seemed more wizened than Mack, more aware. He spoke of history and how important it was, and Mack didn't seem interested in that at all. They were two different people, sure, but Will couldn't help but wonder if it was more than just different interests that stood out. Will wondered if the difference was deeper, more experienced, more grounded...generational.

He didn't have long to think about it.

Every night after the first one, a different dream came to Will. His vantage point was somewhere in the room where they couldn't see him, but he was still part of the action. Will may have called them dreams, but that was only because he didn't have another word to describe them, but he knew they were more than that. He knew that right away and didn't have time to let it frighten him. There was an urgency to them, a buildup he could feel in his very bones. Will needed to pay attention to what was happening in that weird state because not doing so might be the mistake he couldn't take back.

Tired man in checked pants with cuffs that rode high off his shoes, his white sweater vest tight against his flat stomach, walking across the pedestrian path, crossing the bridge with the city lights of Manhattan's upper west side illuminating the sky behind him.

Afroed girl in a yellow tube top and brown and gold striped bell-bottoms riding in the back of a car, eyes wide in the dark of night.

Teenager in stone-washed jeans cuffed at the ankles but otherwise ballooned around his skinny lower half, skulking, trying to stick to the shadows once the cliff presented itself, almost like he would rather scale the rock face than pay the toll.

Man with a high-top fade and a gold herringbone chain

that caught the light driving a black Ford Escort that had seen better days at top speed over the last joint that connected the bridge to asphalt, where it swapped suspension for firm, hard ground... a man who looked suspiciously like me.

All of them, every last one, compressed against the air before crossing properly into New Jersey, their bones broken, crushed, ground against something unseen in that nowhere land between states, dying without a home. *If* they had truly died. Will couldn't tell because before he could make himself look at the gore, the utter mutilation, they were gone, wiped away, like they never existed. No blood, no entrails, no bones. Just nothing. And then he would wake up in a bed soaked through with sweat and a promise on the air that he too would suffer the same fate if he didn't figure out a way.

"Hey man, we gotta go," Will heard himself say to Tip, his lips close enough to touch the man's ear. He didn't remember crossing the room and going out onto the dance floor to break up Tip and Michelle's love fest, but there he was. He could see the disappointment on Tip's face, but didn't stay long enough for the man to think he could ask for more time. They all knew they had to go, that being at the show was just to have an alibi if they needed one. Will hadn't told them everything, hadn't mentioned the dreams to anyone at all because they seemed so off the wall, but they knew there was something big at the end of the bridge, over there in Fort Lee, if they could just find it. But they had to go that night – not during the day, not some other time... that night. The prospect of a big haul kept their mouths closed, which Will had counted on. He hated himself for what he had done and what he was about to do, but there was no time to wallow in that either.

It was time.

The dancers came out hot, bouncing so energetically the makeshift platform buckled and threatened to break. Will wondered if the idea he'd had about the floor caving in had been some kind of premonition. There was yelling in his ears, too. It had been coming to him here and there since the last dream two nights before. But Will assumed it was just his conscious trying to get hold of him for once, to make him change course and do something else. But his mother was dead because of the dreams and Mack and what Mack wanted him to find. She'd tried to stop him, and he'd steamrolled over her a few jumps ago, and he owed. He couldn't remember how long it had been, and that drove him crazy, so he focused on finishing, since that was the only thing he could do. There was no turning back, even if Carl's voice, deep and rich, boomed, "No!" in harmony with every other step Will took.

He needed the dreams to stop.

He needed to finish this for his mother.

He needed to find what Mack wanted him to find.

"But where *exactly* are we headed?" Tip asked from the back seat. They were speeding across the George Washington Bridge, and Tip's arm was curled around Michelle, and Will was happy for him. She was into him – Tip didn't know that yet - he only hoped it was true - but she was. They probably wouldn't ever be able to do anything other than this – hug in the back seat of a cramped car – but at least they'd have that. Michelle's friend Renee had been quiet all night. She was supposed to be there to hang out with Will while Michelle and Tip figured out what they were going to get into, but she and Will had barely spoken two words to each other all night. That was ok. In the end, everything would be.

Will answered the question, thought it was only right. After all, he could already feel the fillings in his teeth wrenching away from the enamel, struggling to get out, stretching, drawing, reaching toward something outside the car as if summoned by a magnet. Soon he'd see the flesh from Renee's face pull away from her skull. He'd watch Tip's eyes pop from their sockets as they followed the same yearning his fillings had. He'd hear the audible slaps their flesh would make as it hit the glass that would be pulsing then, in and out, in and out, like a heartbeat, before it became liquid and overtook Tip's ruined eyes, submerging what was left in an impossible pool of metallic gray and sickly yellow.

Soon.

For now, only his teeth knew what was to come. And they began to ache.

Michelle was oddly quiet, her eyes reflecting the lights that illuminated the bridge like mirrors.

Will started, his voice gravelly, "We're going into Jersey to-"

"I can see that, man," Tip laughed, and something inside Will didn't appreciate being the butt of the joke, just like his dear old cousin, Mack. "What I *don't* get is why we'd leave a bumpin' party right when it was startin' to get hot."

Tip let his hand dip lower than Michelle's shoulder to pet the flesh just above her breast. He thought he was really doing something, but she kept staring at Will with her dead eyes.

"To go to shitty-ass New Jersey."

Tip laughed, but nobody else did. It didn't stop him, though.

"What are we going to *do* in Jersey, pray tell?"

Pray tell? Will thought and fought the urge to shake his head. You could take the rich boy out of the country club, but you couldn't take the country club outta the rich boy.

"There's some money waiting for me there. At Metropolitan Studios."

Will told them everything because it didn't matter. They would never be able to stop him. They would never be able to tell anyone else either, not if his dreams were right.

"Money? *Just* money? Man..." Tip said, as if it were the most ridiculous reason to mess up an otherwise perfect night. "You shoulda said something. We didn't need to drive all the way out here for some *money*. Somebody owe you or something?"

Will stayed silent, listening. He tasted blood in his mouth.

"Man, we coulda taken care of this some other time."

Tip looked over at Michelle, noting where his hand was, and let the corner of his mouth raise in an anticipatory smile he probably thought was charming. He let his gaze linger as he continued.

"I coulda fronted you whatever it was if you needed it like that."

Tip was genuinely upset, and Will could appreciate that. He thought about saying something to placate him but dug the tip of his tongue into the gaping hole one of his fillings had left instead.

"We're all gonna die," Michelle said, her monotone voice filling the cabin as Tip ranted about how he thought there was jewelry and gold and other shit waiting for them out there in Jersey. He said a whole lot of things that didn't make a lot of sense, but it was all background noise to Will. He was entranced by Michelle's words and the faraway look in her eyes.

Will seemed to be the only one who heard her.

When he looked at Michelle, turning in his seat to face her, he noticed that one of her irises had detached and was crumpled over itself in a heap of brown.

Will turned back to the road and smiled. Blood stained his teeth.

"Wait. Will... man, did you say Metropolitan Studios?"

Will didn't trust his voice, so he nodded.

"There *is* no Metropolitan Studios, dude." Tip laughed incredulously as he pulled Michelle closer. All Will heard was, 'Stupid idiot. Stupid nigger. Stupid ass.'

"What?" Will managed and spat blood onto the steering wheel. "What the fuck did you just say?"

"Yo, are you all right?" Tip asked, leaning forward to peer closer at Will and the bloody spit dripping down the center pad of the steering wheel. "Is your nose bleeding or something? I used to get nosebleeds all the ti-"

"What. The. Fuck. Did. You. Say?" Will's voice wasn't much more than a growl.

Tip sat back carefully, keeping his surprised eyes on the back of Will's head.

"I said the studios are gone," he said cautiously, all humor gone from his voice. "That place burned down a long time ago. Decades ago, man. Before our time. Been gone since the 50s, I think."

The lights on the bridge illuminated the cabin of the car like the searchlight of a helicopter, and Michelle's eyes reflected it, shooting it at Will like laser beams.

All white.

All white.

No red.

No cars on this bridge because we're all dead, the voice in Will's head trilled.

Movie magic.

Dead magic.

He should have known...

...would have, but Mack would never believe.

And she was laughing.

"Whoever told you they left money at the studio for you was pulling your leg. There's nothing left of the place."

Will didn't hear Tip tell him that he thought it was a park now, didn't notice when Michelle's voice cracked and broke, nor when she started hitting her head on the glass, thud thud thudding against it until it broke. He heard only Renee because she had started screaming, screaming like she had seen Hell through the split that was opening at the mouth of the bridge, screaming like doing so would save her from the jagged gnashing teeth that waited inside. And then he heard Mack, and he was screaming too.

\/\\|/\\|/
INHERITANCE

To HIS CREDIT, the attempt had been a good one. He'd called Hattie into service faster than she'd been able to find a suitable slave. The argument had really burned him up, so he went home that night and set to the business of concocting his potion. But Hattie had been easy to dissuade, at least thus far. Sharon didn't have to do much more than lock the door against her to keep her at bay. A quick sidestep and the old girl was lost. Wilson hadn't bothered to teach Hattie anything more than how to get up and walk again. He told her to go after Sharon and to kill her, but he hadn't told her how.

Sharon got used to the beating against her front door. Hattie could stay out there all night if she wanted to. It didn't bother Sharon any and there wasn't a neighbor to complain for miles. She figured Wilson would wait until morning to see if Hattie had done the job. After the funeral, just so it would look right. People would wonder why he wasn't in the family car, it being his brother-in-law's funeral and all. They would wonder if he was anywhere except right by his wife's side.

Sharon had time.

Hattie hadn't figured out that she would do better to bust in the windows yet. Sharon doubted that she would. The woman hadn't been a brain surgeon in life. How could Sharon expect her to be any different in death? Sharon sucked her teeth as she walked into the spare bathroom, the room where she brewed her potions and cast her spells. She thought back on how she and Wilson had gotten to the place they were—wanting to kill each other.

Their mother had left the shop to the both of them. She had been a respected woman in their village, a woman who was known to take care of people's problems. Half the time she didn't do anything except sell roots and dried fruit for one potion or the next; she told Sharon and Wilson herself that the whole thing was bogus. But it worked, and she never had to put in a hard day's labor in the hot sun in her life.

Wilson played around with it. 'Momma's mumbo-jumbo,' he called it. He was the oldest and the one who was supposed to inherit the business. He never caught on though, and was easily overshadowed by his younger sister, who seemed to have the real gift. When their mother died, she left everything to the both of them. And that's where the trouble started.

"You're making us look like fools," Sharon said from the back room of the shop that day. "No one will believe us if you keep gallivanting around the street like a commoner."

"They don't believe us as it is, Sharon," he said, tired of the argument. It was always the same thing over and over. "People are smarter now. They know this is a bunch of bullshit."

Sharon burst through the beads that hung from the ceiling to separate the rooms and growled, "Watch your tongue in momma's house."

Wilson chuckled. "Sharon, Momma's been dead for ten years already. When are you gonna cut it out?" He turned his back to his sister and fondled one of the dry herbs that hung from the ceiling.

"Her *ánimo* is still here, Wilson. She's angry that you speak of her that way."

"Right, sure," he said condescendingly. "Anyhow, I just came here to tell you that I'll be talking with a man about selling this dump. I'm gonna try and get whatever money we can out of this place and do something with it. Maybe I'll move to the mainland. Who knows?"

Sharon looked stricken. "You can't sell the place! This is Momma's legacy!"

Wilson flicked the herb and sent it swinging on the string that held it. "It's not much of a legacy, now is it? You can barely live on what we make from it. I have to work a second job just to keep food on the table." He shook his head and stood to leave. "I'm selling it, Sharon. And there's nothing you can do about it."

Wilson walked toward the door, opened it, and turned to speak before leaving. "But you should have already known that, *bruha.*"

Sharon cursed him then, vowing to stop him by any means necessary. She didn't utter a sound as she stood facing the closed door of her mother's shop, but Wilson heard every word.

The church was sticky, and the mosquitoes were relentless. They couldn't resist the bounty they were getting: thirty people crammed into a small church with nothing but their hands to protect them. They feasted.

Wilson escorted his wife in and sat in front of the body of her brother. Clay had been a strong man, muscular and fit for most of his life. He worked out on the boats and was stung by a Portuguese Man of War during an afternoon pull. They didn't make it back to the dock in time to save him after he went into cardiac arrest.

As his wife sobbed, all Wilson could think about was Sharon. She wasn't at the funeral, so she must be dead. She wouldn't have missed Clay's service. She fancied him and was genuinely saddened by his death. Wilson tried to conceal his smile as he thought of Hattie taking Sharon by surprise. She must have been shocked to see her, considering she had attended Hattie's funeral a couple of days earlier. He would talk to the man after they put Clay in the ground, Wilson surmised. He would have his money in less than a month.

His wife's shaking grew intense, and a cry was stuck in her throat, choking her. Wilson turned to her and said, "Honey? Honey, are you ok?" He didn't see Clay fidgeting in his tight casket, didn't recognize the sounds of grunting from his chest and the ripping of the stitches in his lips to be what they were. His wife's eyes were wide open, unblinking, in shock. "Honey?" He shook her slightly, trying to rouse her. She wouldn't look at him.

Wilson turned his head in the direction of his wife's stare in time to see Clay sit up in the casket. An audible moan escaped his chest as the air escaped his lungs. Clay forced his mouth and eyes open, ripping the stitches apart. He lifted his right arm and then his left, inspecting them in disbelief. The whole thing was so much déjà vu to Wilson that he didn't move.

Then Clay climbed out of the casket.

Wilson didn't hear the shrieks and screams that emanated from the congregation as Clay planted his feet on the floor. He only saw Sharon standing at the back of the church, smiling prettily, devilishly.

Clay moved quickly for one of the undead. He closed the space between him and Wilson in three strides and pressed down on his shoulders, buckling his legs, making him submit. Wilson became aware of a pungent odor, the smell of meat that had been left out in the sun. Sharon had converted Hattie in the light of day and brought her along as backup.

With everything he could remember from Momma, with everything he had, he called Hattie inside. She came sluggishly, bewildered. She looked at Sharon, who was too busy watching the show in front of her to notice. Then she looked at Wilson.

He intimated his command to her, deftly breaking Sharon's spell and reinforcing his own. Hattie was upon Sharon before she could turn around.

The smell of fresh blood permeated the air as Hattie ripped away Sharon's scalp. Sharon's scream was nothing more than an afterthought, as was her limp hand against Hattie's decaying cheek. She was dead as soon as her skull was exposed to the summer air. Hattie banged Sharon's head against the wall like a squirrel might a nut and pawed at the brain inside.

Clay smelled the blood just before Wilson did. He turned his head, lessening his grip just enough so that Wilson could slip away. Clay lunged at Sharon, grabbing her leg and digging his nails into her skin, cutting through the flesh and muscle with determined swipes. He licked at the blood that spewed from the wounds before baring his teeth and biting into the supple flesh. Wilson slinked against the wall, trying to make a quiet exit while Hattie and Clay dined on Sharon. He noticed for the first time that the church was empty, including his wife. He'd have to remember that she hadn't tried to help him at all, that she had just left him in there to deal with two zombies. Yes, that was useful information indeed.

Wilson stood in the doorway to watch as Clay sank his teeth into Sharon for another bite, sinews and fatty tissue draped over his working lips. He looked at Sharon's face one last time, at her ruined eyes and what was left of her exposed brain, and smiled. So much for her being the only one who "got it". As he closed the door to the church, he changed his face from satisfaction to fear to please the waiting crowd. His wife ran up to him, tears streaming, wetting her cheeks. He hoped she couldn't see the hatred in his eyes.

He'd meet the man later that day. He'd have his money in less than a month.

Dear Monique,

Hey girl! It's been a while since we've talked—well, a while for us is anything more than 3 days! I can't believe we've remained so close for over 30 years! I can remember the day we met at McAllen Day School. Nicole, the bully, was picking on you, and I felt a jolt of assuredness—don't ask me how or why. I marched my little self right up to that mountain of a girl and told her to get away from you (oh, by the way, I saw Nicole this week in California. She was at the convention I went to. She looks great. Even though I've got about 20 pounds on her now, I still felt a little twang of dread when we recognized each other!). I told her that you were my sister, remember? We don't look anything like each other, then or now. You with your long blonde hair and piercing green eyes and me with my dark-brown locks and copper-toned skin. Who did I think I would be fooling? But I got Nicole off you that day, and we've been friends ever since.

Wow! Can you believe it's been just over 30 years? Through junior high and realizing that boys existed for something other than to annoy us (I'm still not too sure about that J), to high school and going on our first dates. You went out with that jerk, Tommy Kern. What a bum! I thought he was a bum then, only I didn't want to tell you that. Even though we had been friends practically all of our lives, you were so into Tommy that I was afraid to let you know how I felt about him. I thought you would hate me for it, so I kept it to myself. Things worked out for the best, though. Right after you broke up with Tommy, the loser, you met Greg, dear sweet Greg.

My choices in high school weren't much better than yours. I dated Calvin and Robert – two jerks who never should have gotten the time of day from me. I went to the prom with a friend of mine because Calvin and I had called it quits two weeks before. I still can't believe that! What timing! Remember Will? I had a crush on Will for years! We grew up with him from McAllen Elementary all the way to college. He was a year older than we were and fine as all hell, so I thought it would be a cool stinger to bring a college man to the prom with me. A <u>fine</u> college man. And it worked! I got Calvin good! I'll never forget how his face looked when I walked in on Will's arm. Ooh girl, do you remember just how fine Will looked in that tux??? He was a vision...until we went into the city to party after the prom. He drank the whole way down! When we got to the club, I practically had to hold him up so he didn't fall on his face. I have never been more embarrassed. That was the worst possible prom night anyone could ever have.

College wasn't that much better than high school for me, was it? We followed each other to UCLA. Even though you two were across the country from each other, you and Greg were still hooked up. I still can't believe you didn't date anyone else during college. I mean, we were only 20ish—prime time for dating around and experimenting. I can't believe you gave up all of that. But when I take a look at the man you gave it up for, I can't say that I wouldn't have done the same if I were in your shoes. Greg was a wonderful man, Monique. A truly wonderful man.

Let's see, I dated Rick, Troy, Nigel, and Michael my first year. Not too shabby. Second year, I dated another Rick, William, Bradley, Travis, Ronald, and Steve, right? Or was Shaun that year too? Third year is when the love bug bit me. It was when we went down to Huntington Beach that Friday night to hang out. We were staying with Carol in Irvine for the weekend, and we wanted to get some good seafood. You and I went to Huntington thinking more like we were going to City Island in New York. I was craving shrimp like the ones that are served up at the end of City Island's restaurant strip. To this day, I haven't found anything like it.

Anyway, we went down there and ate at some joint that wasn't worth the trip, and then we took a stroll on the beach. You spotted him first, remember? He was walking along the beach with some girl. They looked like they were having a really intense conversation about something. I remember that he looked annoyed. His brow was furrowed, and his shoulders were hunched. But when he looked over at us, his eyes softened. I should say when he looked at you, really. At least, that's what I always thought. I always thought that he was checking you out that night on the beach. It probably sounds really silly coming from me after all of these years, but I did... and still do.

I don't know. Something about the air out here makes me go back in time. I can see it all like it just happened. We were on the beach; they walked by us, and we turned our heads. He is as attractive now as he was then. Tall, muscular, smooth, deep chocolate skin; he was breathtaking! I was nervous. I was never the kind to approach a guy and try to start a conversation. Eye contact still bothers me sometimes. It's so intense. But you, well, you never really had that problem, did you? You looked at him like he should have been privileged to be walking on the same beach that we were. You turned your head with a quick little twist; your hair floating in the breeze lightly; almost like it was being carried in slow motion. And he kept looking at you. He just kept looking.

I swear, had it not been for you pushing me off on him, he would never have taken a second glance at me. I mean it! But thank goodness you did step aside and let him see me for me. It took a little time before I really let him break the shell, but when I did, I gave him my all. That's what I don't under-stand about this, Monique.

I remember the day we met Greg. He was playing basketball in the gym. I remember the gym being hot and muggy all the time. Muggy and smelly, like old shoes. We were walking to the track for cheerleading practice. It was our day to do laps (oh joy) and we were dreading it like usual. I went to the water fountain to get a drink, and I thought you were right behind me. When I turned around, you were still at the gym doors peering through the glass. You looked like a lost puppy. You should have seen yourself! Greg was practicing his foul line shot, and he was totally engrossed in it. But that didn't matter to you. Every move he made, every dribble, every pause, every shot you followed with immense intensity. It was almost like you were holding your breath with each release of the ball. I'll never forget the way your face lit up and then turned beet red when he looked over at the gym doors and spotted you gawking at him. He smiled cockily and turned back to his practice. You were on cloud nine! It was all you would talk about for months! It got so bad that I was wishing he would just ask you out already so I could stop hearing about how great Greg was. And he did.

It seems like we're always there for each other's spectacular moments. Like when I had Jessica. You were the first person aside from Russell to see her. She adores you, just like we do. I always thought it was a shame that you and Greg weren't able to have any children. I know that you guys had been talking about adopting—what ever happened to that? I think it would be a wonderful idea, especially now that Greg is gone. You need someone to keep you company, to keep you busy. I worry about you, Monique. I really do.

I know it just sounds like I'm rambling on and on in this letter. I've just got so much on my mind right now that I need to talk to you about. I mean, it's really only one thing, but it seems so massive, so intangible, and I really need you to help me put this into perspective. I don't want to lose control the way other women do. I don't want to be like them. I just don't want it to seem like this has shattered my life. But it does, doesn't it? I mean, after all, things will change—must change—as a result of this. I guess I _am_ like those women who completely fold up and crumble when this kind of thing happens. I share two things in common with them: I never thought this could happen to me, for one, and then it did; and no matter what I did to prevent it or how much I tried to block it out, it happened. I know it did, Monique; I know it happened. It happened, and God help us all.

Russell has never been happy with the amount of traveling that I do, you know. He has always said that it was going to cause problems if it got out of hand, and I have been traveling more than usual this year. I guess that's what you could call 'out of hand.' But Monique, the business has really been booming this year. I have to travel to take care of my clients. Their needs are growing, and I have to be able to accommodate them all if I want to keep them. I have to go to any training opportunity available if I plan to remain competitive, right? Cutting edge is the name of the game, and I have to be able to convince my clients that I am on that cutting edge, if not defining it, or they won't stay with me. Do you know what I mean? Of course not! You have the luxury of not having to work. Greg left you a very nice nest egg when he passed away so suddenly. Trust me, Monique, you wouldn't want to be out here in this dog-eat-dog world. The competition is fierce, and sometimes I want out too, but when I come home and see my little girl's face grinning up at me, I know why I'm doing it all. At least, that's my rationale for now.

That being said, I have to work like this. Russell's job is decent, but the growth potential is not substantial. Mine is, so I do it. Well, for the past couple of months, he has been acting really funny. Different, you know what I mean? For a long time, I couldn't put my finger on exactly what it was. For a long time, he was pretty good at hiding it. He would do little things, you know? Things out of the ordinary but not big enough to raise any flags on their own. Sometimes he wouldn't be home when I got in from work. Now you know I don't set foot in the door until at least 7:30 p.m. every night, and he is usually back with Jessica by 6:00, so that struck me as odd. It only happened a couple of times, but it happened, and when you're dealing with a man who prides himself on being so routine you could set your clock by him, it looks a little funny. I mean, he always had a good reason for not being there. Once he said he had taken Jessica shopping, but there weren't any bags (she didn't like anything, he said. She's 5 years old! She likes everything she sees!), or the time when they went to see the clown in the town center. Ok, maybe, but I don't know... something really bothered me about his behavior. But I never said anything – what could I say? Then, when I was away on business, he would come home really late at night. I mean, I assumed he was coming home late. All I know is that he would be wide awake at 11:45 p.m. when I would call in a last-ditch effort to speak to him. He would be awake and sound right chipper, too. That's not like him. Russell usually gets in bed at 10:00 p.m. on the nose. It's been that way for years. It just didn't make sense to me. When I would ask him what he was doing up so late, some-times he would say that he had been doing some reading. Another one he frequently used was that he heard Jessica stir, and he had just come back from checking on her. That never happens when I'm home. It just seemed odd.

I know you think I'm overreacting, but I'm not. I know what I know. There's more to this than what I've told you so far. When I came home, he would be really nice, almost too nice. Know what I mean? He would shower me with flowers and kind words, so much so it became nauseating. He knows that I can't stand too much of that sappy stuff. If you say I love you too many times in a day, it makes my skin crawl. I'm not like most women. I don't like all that togetherness, that all over you, got to touch you kind of love. I just don't and never have. Russell knows that about me. But yet and still, he is all over me like I'm the best thing going when I get home. Like he has been waiting all his life to lay eyes on me. Monique, Russell didn't used to be so hot to see me when I came home. He never used to be so affectionate. I asked him once what got into him. I didn't want to hurt his feelings, but all that touching was getting on my nerves. He said that he just loved me, and he wanted to make things right. I told him that things were right; at least they were the last time I checked. He said that he wanted things to be the way they were before, and then he hugged me fiercely. I was pinned in his embrace. I couldn't move. For a second, I thought I was going to suffocate. I know you think what I'm saying is cruel and callous but that's the kind of stuff you go for, not me. I remember that Greg used to shower you with trinkets and tidbits, and you just ate it up like it was candy. Me, show me your strength, your integrity, not your taste in jewelry. That's what does it for me. I thought that was what Russell was all about.

So, as you can imagine, I was really suspicious

of Russell by that point. I checked his drawers and didn't find anything out of the ordinary. I swear to you, Monique, I don't know exactly what I was looking for. Something, anything that would clue me in to some devious act. What that something was, I didn't know. A number, perfume on his clothes, lipstick on his collar; I didn't know. I wasn't ready for it to be what it was, though. Nothing could have prepared me for that.

About a week ago, I came home early from my appointment in Rockville. I went into the house, and nothing looked out of the ordinary. Russell was home; he was upstairs in the shower. I came in, yelled hello, and went into the kitchen. My usual routine. See, at this point I was just thinking my husband was acting freaky, not anything else, especially when I hadn't found anything substantial to use against him. I hadn't formed any ideas in my head about what could be happening other than maybe he was going through some thirty-something crisis, which was a mild version of what was waiting for him during the real middle-aged crisis. Just a preview of what was to come. I hadn't concocted any scenarios on this yet. I swear I hadn't.

I went into the kitchen and saw two plates, two glasses, and some silverware in the sink. Nothing strange about that. I had some toast with my banana that morning, so I walked right by the sink nonchalantly, assuming that Russell hadn't had the time to put the dishes in the dishwasher after I left. I pulled out a glass from the cabinet, got some cranberry juice from the refrigerator, and drank it down quickly. I put the glass in the sink and got ready to run some water so that I could rinse the dishes and put them in the dishwasher. That's when I saw it. I don't know how I saw this. The lighting wasn't right—remember it was really rainy a week ago—and I wasn't looking for anything, but lo and behold, there it was, as clear as day. I picked up the fork that was in the sink and looked at it closely. What had caught my eye was the pale, frosted pink smear of lipstick left on that fork. Pale frosted pink lipstick that I do not wear. I am strictly earth reds and browns, Monique, reds and browns. Not pale pink. Never pale pink. And just like that, Russell appeared in the kitchen. God, it took everything I had not to throw the fork at him or say something damning. But I didn't. I didn't! He came to me and hugged me tightly, and you know what? I took that hug. I hugged him back, girl. I hugged him and dropped that fork into the sink like it was hot metal. Russell jumped when he heard the fork clink against the plates in the sink, and I think he realized then that I had seen it. He nudged me out of the way lightly but deliberately and immediately turned the water on, destroying the evidence of that pale pink frosted lipstick. I couldn't keep the smile off my face. It was a poisonous smile, one that could have bored holes right through him if given the chance, but I made it as sweet as possible. Do you understand that right then and there I realized that my husband, the man I had trusted my life to, the man I trusted my child's life to, was a cheating bastard? At that moment, my world changed dramatically.

I let him clean the dishes, and I went upstairs and took a shower of my own. I put on my soft robe and snuggled on the bed watching the tape of my soap opera. I couldn't even focus. I picked up a book and tried to read a little, but I couldn't do that either. My mind kept running over his behavior in my head. Over and over again I saw him being really fidgety when alone with me, being overly animated when I came back from a trip, and then today, using every ounce of willpower he had to keep himself in check when he knew I saw that fork. It all made sense. There was another woman; there had to be. That son of a bitch had gotten himself a whore to fuck him when I'm gone. Monique, I work like a dog to get us in a position where we don't have to work for the rest of our lives. I wanted us to be able to watch Jessica grow up rather than work and miss it all. He just works his same job day to day. He takes no initiative to get moving, move up in the ranks; he's content. Damn it, if he didn't let me be the man! That bastard!

Well, I remembered that pale pink frosted whore's color. That afternoon, after I picked Jessica up from kindergarten, we went to the mall. I went to two or three beauty counters and looked for something that matched it. I found a lot of things that came really close—Poppy, Raspberry, even Mostly Mauve. I didn't find the actual color until the next day on my lunch hour. I went to a different mall, and I saw it. Mattehorn. I bought a tube of it and took it home. I tried it on my hand and forearm, trying desperately to remember the color on the fork. I wanted to make sure that I had the right lipstick. If I didn't, my plan wouldn't work. I put the color on my lips anyway, thinking that if it didn't work and I had the wrong color, it would go in the cabinet with all the other colors that I've bought over time that I don't like but can't bear to throw away. I put it on and lined my lips nicely. The color was nice enough on the right woman. A woman with considerably lighter skin and hair could probably carry it off much better than I could. It made my lips look like they were taking over my face. The urge to take it off and scrub my face clean was about to overcome me when Russell came home, late again. He usually ran up the stairs like a bat out of hell so that he could get to the restroom to unwind. But today he seemed to be dilly-dallying for a while. Just add that to the list of strange behaviors he had been displaying for the past couple of months. I called down to him and asked him to come up. He did, taking the stairs methodically, almost as if he was counting them one by one. He came to the bathroom door and looked at me in the mirror. His eyes squinted as they fixed themselves on my lips, as pink and bubbly as they were, set in a sappy sweet smile that would have charmed any man. He looked a little while longer before saying something like, 'Honey, is that a new lip color?'. Something pitiful like that came out of his mouth. I played along with his little game. I told him that I went to the store, and it jumped out at me, but that I wasn't all that sure. I still liked it. I told him that you had it and I wanted to try it, but that it doesn't look good on me. Come to think of it, that's not really a lie. You wear this color, don't you? Mattehorn. It sounds familiar. I thought that then. Maybe you'll want this tube of barely used lipstick when this is all over.

That night went smoothly. To be honest with you, my mind wasn't really there. I had to leave and come out here to California the next day, and I really couldn't wait. I felt like I would spill the beans if I stayed. I didn't want to just come out and tell him that I thought he was cheating on me without some kind of proof. I mean, yeah, the lipstick is a little bit of proof, but that's a pretty thin piece of evidence, don't you think? It could have been anyone's lipstick! That doesn't account for his strange behavior, though, but that's all perception. I needed something real. So, I left for California to come to this dry-ass conference. Not exactly the thing I needed while I plotted how to find out if my husband was being untrue, but I guess it will have to do.

After two days, I couldn't take it anymore. I had to find out something somehow. I came home early. I came home on Thursday instead of Sunday. I stayed at a cheap motel on the outskirts of town so that no one would know. I wanted to catch him so badly, Monique, and I did.

I went up to the house one night and hid in the woods. I felt really stupid, seeing as it was my own property that I was slinking around on, but I did it anyway. Part of me didn't think that he would be stupid enough to bring the bitch to our house with Jessica being there, but hell, he'd done it before, hadn't he? My car was parked three blocks over, so there's no way he could have spotted me, and I was wearing all black. You know how thick our woods are. No one would ever see me out there. I stood there for two hours before anything happened, but

*then something did happen. My God, I never
thought it would be—.*

Monique's hands shook as she read the letter. She tore her eyes away and looked up at the sky. She had been frozen in place, standing in her driveway reading the letter for God knows how long. She couldn't believe what she was reading! There was no way it could be true. She distantly heard herself reaffirming that over and over out loud; convincing herself that it simply wasn't possible.

"Oh, but it is possible, Monique."

The voice came from behind her, close behind her. She could feel the breath on her neck, hot and sour. She could hear the belabored breathing and the crazed wheezing that rose lightly with each exhale. She was terrified. She shook as she turned towards the familiar voice. The voice of her friend. The voice of a woman who was beyond the edge of her sanity.

"Christine, what—."

"Don't talk, Monique. Just read. Read it out loud so I can hear you say the words. I want to hear you say them. But let's go inside first. No need to let the world in on our business, is there?"

Monique felt the muzzle of a gun press firmly against the small of her back, and she jumped. Christine smiled, satisfied with the fear emanating from her pores, wafting the tinny smell of adrenaline to her nostrils. She continued,

"Good. Now let's go inside."

Monique turned slowly towards the door and walked cautiously. She wanted to run and hide, but she knew Christine wouldn't allow her to get too far. Christine was in better shape than she was and Christine had always been stronger than she was, both mentally and physically. She knew she had no chance to get away.

She opened the side door and walked inside, followed closely by Christine. She sat down at the kitchen table and waited. Christine shut the door and locked it. She walked around the kitchen holding the gun lackadaisically and said,

"No, we're not going to read the rest of the letter here. We're going to read it in the bedroom. I've always liked your bedroom."

Monique looked up at Christine, who was standing over her, piercing her with eyes full of hatred. She said meekly,

"Why are you doing this, Christine?"

Christine snickered and said,

"Just get up, Monique. You'll understand everything in a little while."

Monique got up from the chair and started up the stairs to her bedroom. She was scared to death of what Christine might do to her and also of what she might do to herself. She had never seen her so out of control.

Monique opened her bedroom door and saw Russell tied up and gagged. He had been shot in the head twice, and there was coagulated blood on his face and shirt. Monique screamed and dropped the letter on the floor. She turned to run, but Christine shoved her onto the bed. She fell on top of Russell's mutilated body and came close to passing out.

"Read the rest of the letter," Christine ordered.

Monique jerked her body away from Russell's oddly warm corpse and onto the edge of the bed. She groped for the letter on the floor, afraid to take her eyes off Christine. She found the letter and brought it slowly up to eye level.

Christine sat in the rocking chair next to the bedroom door with the gun pointed at Monique with a lazy arm.

"Read it now, Monique," she said coarsely, making herself comfortable in the chair that she had given Monique just before she and Greg lost their baby. "Read it to Russell."

Monique's face crumbled as she looked at Russell lying dead on her bed. She looked back at Christine with pleading eyes.

"That's right," Christine said coldly, "Face Russell and read the letter to him. I think it's only fair that he hears it, too. Anyway, I can't stand looking at you anymore."

Monique turned around and looked at Russell reluctantly, her back turned to Monique. A sob rose in her throat, and she choked it back. Her eyes took in the sight of her murdered lover. His skin was drained of color already, his normally rich brown skin taking on grayish blue overtones. It made her sick. She couldn't bear to look at his ruined face.

Christine grew impatient.

"Get on with it," she shouted. "Start where you left off."

Monique swallowed hard; her throat had become desperately dry. She cleared her throat loudly and dramatically. Christine rolled her eyes and waved the gun in the air. Monique's voice came out in a whisper at first.

*—My God, I never thought it would be you.
How could it be you? Can you tell me, Monique?
How could it be you? How could you sneak around
behind my back after all our years of friendship?
After all the love I have shown you, how could you
sleep with my husband? I should have killed you*

both right then and there. I almost did. When I saw him kiss you at the front door and pull you into the house, I was sick. I looked through the window and saw the two of you groping at each other like two dogs in heat. It was disgusting! Downright nasty...but sensuous. I didn't know that watching you two could turn me on. It got me thinking about how Greg's hands felt on my body, and how intense he looked when he was really aroused. I used to like it when he would just rip my clothes off me and smack me on the ass nice and hard –.

Monique's head jerked up, and her fiery eyes turned to Christine, who was sitting in the chair with her hand on the rim of her unbuttoned jeans. Monique's lips snarled as Christine turned her head back in erotic, contemptuous laughter. Monique's anger filled her completely, blinding her to the situation at hand. Her body tensed as she prepared to lunge at Christine. Before she could move, Christine held up the gun and said,

"Not so fast. We're not done yet. Read the rest."

Christine smiled evilly, amused at the surge of anger adding color to Monique's cheeks. After snickering under her breath, she said,

"Go on, read it, bitch."

Monique sat down slowly, enraged at what she had read, wanting to rip Christine apart with her bare hands. She picked up the letter and continued reading through her clenched teeth.

—Yeah, when I think about Greg, it makes me really hot. I couldn't help but think of how ironic this is. I mean, I trusted you all my life, and you slept with my husband. That was something that, up until then, I had been feeling pretty bad about doing to you. Well, that's not the only reason I had been feeling bad. I felt bad about the whole thing, really.

There were so many times that I wanted to tell you about it, but how do you tell someone that you had their husband murdered by mistake? There was no easy way to do it. But now I think you deserve to know. Greg wanted to call it off. He wanted to leave me and go back to you. He said his conscience was killing him and that he couldn't deceive you anymore. Well, I didn't want him to do it. You know what kind of man Greg was! He was wonderful! He was a great cook, considerate but not nauseating, and a great fuck. I wanted him to be mine for as long as we could keep it a secret. I didn't want him as my husband. I didn't want to confuse Jessica and, truthfully, I didn't want to hurt you. So, I thought I could keep him on a string for as long as I wanted to. But he changed his mind.

When it came time to let him go, I couldn't. We met in the city and grabbed a bite to eat downtown. He told me he wanted to leave. I said no, on and on, and then he got up and walked out. Well, I just couldn't let him go. I got angry. I found some bums that wanted a fix so bad they would have killed their mother if they had to. I paid them to tail him to Metro Center and take him down for me. I told them that he was carrying a lot of money and jewelry, so it would be a good score. I tailed the bums to make sure they got the right guy.

They caught him a block or so away from the train station. They pulled him into an alley and rifled through his things. They had knocked him unconscious by the time I got there. I peeked my head in quickly and kept walking. I couldn't afford to be caught down there while they were mugging him. I don't know; I guess they got carried away. The next thing I knew, you were calling me, saying that Greg was dead.

At first, I didn't believe you. I knew what happened in the city, but he looked alive when I saw him. I guess I was wrong. The coroner said that he suffered extensive wounds to the head as a result of being hit with a blunt object. That's really too bad, Monique. If he had cooperated with me, *this would never have happened to him. I cried as hard as you did at the funeral because I, too, had lost a wonderful man.*

So now you know everything. My slate is clean, and I have nothing else to share. I have something else to give you, though, dear friend. Turn around. It's ready for you.

With love,
Christine

Monique lowered the letter slowly and turned around to face Christine. Christine was standing with the gun pointed at Monique's head, a sardonic smile dancing on her lips. She chuckled and said,

"Good. I wanted you to be looking at me when I did this. Goodbye, old friend."

Monique threw her hands up to try and knock the gun away, but she was too late. The bullet ripped through her forehead with frightening accuracy. Monique fell limply onto the bed, her eyes staring blankly at Christine while the pages of the letter fluttered to the floor, splattered with blood.

With a sigh, Christine closed the door quietly behind her, got in her car, and drove toward Jessica's school to pick her up.

. . .

\\|/\\|/

MALADY

The air was thick, stifling, oppressive. Heavy with water. Her body felt so weak, she could hardly stand. Darkness covered the place so completely, nothing could be seen for miles ahead or right in front of her. It was comprehensive, like blindness, unyielding and whole. A shriek welled in Sabrina's throat, though she dared not utter it.

She took a step forward, needing to feel the familiar press and pull of her flesh as she moved, needing to feel anything at all aside from the air, so palpable it felt like a hand caressing her cheek. But there was nothing. If the step had moved her forward or backward, she couldn't tell. The nothingness in the new space was the same as the nothingness where she stood before.

Sabrina stayed silent for what seemed like hours, her eyes darting to and fro, trying to make out buildings or cars or people walking along a sidewalk. That's what she should have been able to see: a bustling New York City street lined with skyscrapers and crowded with people in a rush to get to a restaurant, a meeting, or to a cab. Whatever the reason, it should have been happening. But it wasn't. She didn't hear the familiar beeping of a cabby's horn as he darted in and out of traffic. She didn't hear the *clicking* and *smacking* of shoes on the sidewalk as the mob walked from one end of the city block to the other. Instead, she heard nothing. Saw nothing. Sabrina started to wonder if she herself was nothing, as everything around her had become.

Was this death? It certainly could have been, given the silence of it all. But when? How? Sabrina remembered being on the street, heading toward the corner. She needed to get to a building a few blocks over for an appointment, and she was late. She was running... did she trip and fall? Did she dart out into traffic and get hit? She wondered if she might have remembered something if that had happened. A flash of light or the screeching of tires, maybe. But she couldn't remember anything other than being on the sidewalk.

Did people just drop dead?

Sabrina's breathing hitched, startling her. She didn't have the impression she was breathing at all, especially with the concept of death floating around in her head. She tried to take a deep breath but couldn't. She tried again but got even less air in her lungs than before. She gasped, beginning to feel starved of air, like she was choking. She *was* choking; something in her mind affirmed it. She was lying on the city street choking while people walked by, too busy to stop and help her. An old lady was sitting on the ground with her, holding her head up and shouting for someone to get help. A homeless man ambled over to look at her with morbid curiosity shining in his eyes. He gazed lasciviously at her legs, more of which was showing as her skirt was hiked up from the fall. He wanted to touch her, and he would as soon as no one was looking. Saliva dripped from his discolored lips and onto her heaving chest. Her purse garnered that reaction; the bum had hit the jackpot.

Sabrina gasped again, trying to suck in elusive air that stubbornly blew away from her. It moved the hair on her forehead and chilled the sweat that glistened on her face, but wouldn't travel to her lungs, wouldn't give her sustenance. A scream pushed through her closing throat, forcing its way out into the air to cut at it for its betrayal. As it crescendoed from her diaphragm with all the force she could muster, Sabrina's eyes flung open. The sound of her scream echoed loudly off the walls of her darkened bedroom, surprising her with the intensity of it; the sound of her fear was raw and shrill. And then there was silence.

The radio Sabrina had left on had been turned off, and though she found that odd, it wasn't the only thing that caught her attention. Kramer, her golden retriever, sat on the floor at the foot of her bed. He rose up on his haunches to look at her as she sat up, jarred from his sleep and desperately wanting to return to it. Sabrina looked at him, love filling her up as his sleepy eyes blinked slowly and he rested his head on the mattress.

"Kramer," Sabrina whispered, her voice thick from sleep and emotion, "what are you doing here, sweetie?"

Kramer blinked again, even slower. A tear cascaded down Sabrina's cheek.

She heard the top step creak under the weight of a foot and smiled. She knew what he was going to say before he said it and was tempted to recite the line for him.

"Honey, what are you doing up?" Jeff started, as he always did on Saturday nights. "I thought you'd be asleep by now. I fell asleep downstairs." Jeff leaned down to kiss Sabrina on the forehead. She raised herself up to meet his lips as tears streamed down her face. She wanted so badly to turn the light on, to see Jeff and Kramer without the obstruction of shadows, but she knew she couldn't. She never could. *Maybe this time will be different*, she told herself. *This time I choked first.*

\/\\\/\|/\|/\\\|/

THE EVER AFTER

1

Oh my God.

I couldn't stop myself from screaming. I had been screaming since it started. I breathed in and out, in and out, only vaguely registering the odd taste of the air, the sulfuric smell.

Dead.

I must be dead. Surely, after a fall from so high, no one could have survived. I looked around at the bodies that littered the field, legs askance, arms bent at impossible angles, and I nodded. We're all dead.

My eyes watered as I looked up at the brilliant blue sky. I was up there. A shiver ran through me as I remembered. It was midday, maybe two or three o'clock – exactly the time when I always start to feel restless at my desk. I wanted the day to be over. I wanted to go out in the sunshine and play. Sometimes I wondered if I was really cut out to work in an office. The walls seemed to close in on me. I couldn't focus, didn't want to think. I hated my cube walls. I hated my office mates.. I hated the work. So uninteresting. So unimportant. I wanted to do something real, something that mattered.

I was on the way outside for my normal break (I took five every day even though I don't smoke) and I was itching to get outside. I passed people I knew in the hall and mumbled hello, shared the elevator with someone and engaged in the obligatory chitchat, then barely stopped myself from running out of the front door.

"Enjoy your break."

That's what he said. Enjoy your break. Such a normal comment, a throwaway, something you really don't mean but you say just to be nice. It's like when people say, 'Have a good day!' or 'How are you?' They don't really want a response; they don't want to listen to some long, drawn-out story. They just needed something to say. *Enjoy your break.* If he hadn't said it, I would have escaped the image of what he would become.

"Enjoy your break," said the guard whose name I never knew. His smile was genuine enough, but he wasn't even looking at me when he said it. He had already moved on to the next person, addressing someone else from his cramped little room. I was just another faceless person to speak to as they passed in and out of the lobby. I smiled back anyway, a thin-lipped thing that could just as easily have been a grimace. And that's when it happened.

Gravity gave way.

First my hair lifted off my head and rose above me like a crown, then my feet lifted off the ground. What I felt was confirmed by what I saw; the guard, several inches taller than me, rose off the ground and struck the low ceiling of his security shack before he could even scream. Instead of stopping, he pressed through, breaking into the ceiling. There was a horrible sound - a wet, cracking, popping noise. Blood, bone, and matter rained down in a torrent from the hole he created.

Oh, my God.

In one wild instant, I caught a glimpse of the world below me. My purse had fallen off my shoulder and was lying on the ground. Papers and pencils littered the guard's desk, splattered with his blood. None of those things were floating up to oblivion. This wasn't gravity giving way. This was something else.

I screamed for the guard as much as for myself. It was only after hearing my own voice that I realized I was moving toward the higher ceiling of the lobby and toward that poor man's same fate. I grabbed the doorframe and pulled myself outside, ducking through with barely enough time to clear the rest of my body before colliding with the doorframe. For the briefest of moments, I tried to will my feet down to the ground, but there was no chance. It was as if I was on an invisible lift being raised up. My ascent was beyond my control.

People outside rose with me, some above me, some below me, some in sync with me. The ascent wasn't quick, and that was the torture of it; the ride was slow enough for me to take in what was happening, just long enough for me to become afraid. Smoke from car accidents below billowed up to us, giving chase. There was so much screaming and crying. Some cursing. Lots of praying. People tried to move toward each other, craving touch, a hand to hold as we rose to our deaths. Surely that's what we were doing – rising to our deaths. Soon we wouldn't be able to breathe, or we'd freeze to death or...

I laughed through my tears. Leave it to me to forget which would happen first. Jenny the airhead forever. Never taking anything seriously. But this was serious all right. It was the end of the world.

Windows broke, and people rose through them, bloodied. Glass protruded out of open wounds, heads cut open to reveal the smooth sheen of bone. Severed heads and detached limbs rose from the crashes below, bobbing on the wind like grotesque Macy's parade floats.

Babies cried. Perhaps that was the worst part.

The air started to get cold, and I began to understand with unwanted clarity that it wouldn't be long now. If gravity kicked in at this point, the drop would crush me. If I didn't stop rising, I would freeze to death. If I escaped that death, somehow, I would not be able to breathe outside of Earth's atmosphere. That's the order, I realized after all. Crazily, I wondered if a spaceship would pick me up? Would I stop on a cloud and see my grandmother waiting there? Delirium had already begun to set in.

My life had been aimless, a collection of unfulfilled dreams and wishful thinking. And now it was over. I cried for myself - for what I wanted to do but hadn't, for the pain I would surely feel when I met my end, regardless of how. I shut my eyes to the terrifying world before me and opened them to this one with the strange blue sky above my head and rough grass beneath me. People lay scattered on the ground, lifeless, except the ones who sat ramrod straight, looking up at the sun with unblinking, inky eyes.

When I sat up under that freakishly blue sky, they all turned to look at me.

2

I wasn't going to cut her.

The thought greeted me as I woke up in the comically green crabgrass. Even as it flitted away, out of my grasp, I knew it was a lie. I meant to cut her and had wanted to from the moment I knew I was ready to leave. I just didn't have the guts to do it.

But I did it, didn't I?

I saw the knife in my hand, saw myself raising it above my head and thrusting it down fast. I heard Felicia yelling at me in that condescending way until she felt the blade pierce her skin. Then she screamed in pain. And fear.

I remember liking that part most of all.

I remember telling her that I couldn't take it anymore, that she needed to act like a woman and not a man. I already have a man, and he knew his role. She needed to learn hers. But she wouldn't. When I wanted her, it was because I craved soft, sexy, alluring: pretty, damn it. Not bossy, foul-mouthed, and rough.

She wasn't always that way. When we started seeing each other, she was sweet and loving. Her face lit up when she saw me. She used to call me Brandy when I hit it right. But when I met Paul and brought him home - when I kissed Paul before kissing her - she changed. She was waiting; I knew that. She was waiting for me to choose her over Paul. She pretended to like our three-way romance and probably did enjoy the sex if she didn't think about it too much. But she wanted me for herself, and not having me made her mad and mean.

Cutting her meant I had chosen. Finally.

My apartment was covered in blood. The walls were splashed with it as I chased her around. Once I started cutting, I had to finish, but she wouldn't stay still. I was on top of her when it happened, making sure she was dead. Her body was warm between my legs. Her little titties were pushed together in her bra, teasing me for the last time.

I should have fucked her one more time before I killed her.

I was thinking that when the sky fell.

It seemed like a cutaway for a TV show; my vision went all white for a second and then gradually came back, showing me this new, weird world. What I saw when I opened my eyes didn't make sense. People were staggering, leaning, falling over. I saw bodies on the ground - some were moving, but others were still. Most people were just staring up at that crazy sky. I looked too - I felt like I was being hypnotized. My body rocked, moving like a dandelion in the breeze. I imagined that my head was like the white fuzz on a dandelion with seeds blowing off in the wind. My hair, nose, and ears blew off too, twisting and turning in the wind and leaving droplets of blood on the ground.

That image is what snapped me out of it – whatever 'it' was.

I looked down, certain I would see Felicia beneath me, her chest destroyed by that piece of shit knife I used on her. I was covered in blood, had to be; I could almost feel it coating my arms. But there wasn't any blood at all. No knife either. And Felicia was nowhere to be found.

I was kneeling in grass with thick, curly lime-greenish blades that seemed to creep toward me in the wind, like they wanted to wrap around my ankles. I shook my head and laughed at myself as I stood up, only distantly wondering where these crazy thoughts were coming from. I felt a lot of things at the moment, but the main thing was relief. And power.

I felt fucking awesome.

I killed my lady ('that bitch' seemed too harsh a name for her now) and got away with it. It was all cleaned up and left behind. It didn't matter that this new place didn't seem real. It didn't freak me out that the grass and the sky – the fucking sun - looked more like a kid's finger painting than something of this world. I didn't even give a shit that there was a guy on the other side of a tree that seemed like it came out of an animated Halloween special staring right at me with eyes that looked like black holes. I just figured it was part of the crazy-ass hallucinations I was having.

Fuck it – I'm free!

No blood- maybe it was all a dream. The thought made me laugh. It couldn't be true; I remembered how warm and slick her blood felt on my hands before waking up in this weird place too well for it to be my imagination but go with it for a second. Maybe Felicia wasn't dead. Maybe I didn't even attack her – who gives a damn? All I care about right now is that she's gone, which means the shit is over.

Amidst all the screaming and whining, I laughed like I had never laughed before.

3

I knew that life the way I knew it had irreversibly changed the moment I saw a corpse driving a car. I also knew I was tripping, but not so hard that I didn't know a dead man when I saw one. The man behind the wheel of a red Subaru that had seen better days was middle-aged, and his chin sported fresh stubble. His old-fashioned wire-rim glasses were perched on his nose. There wasn't anything discernibly wrong with him, not at first glance. He looked like a regular guy driving around town on a sunny day. Except this 'regular guy' couldn't be driving around today, or ever again for that matter. I knew that because my mom went to his funeral just a couple of days ago.

Get your shit together, Carrie.

I sat up taller, took a deep breath, and put both hands on the wheel, trying to shake off what had to be the result of some bad Spice. I'll never buy shit from that asshole Tyler again.

Mr. Ridley nodded as I coasted next to him, coming dangerously close to hitting the Subaru and giving it (and him) the burial it deserves. Some of the lines that had etched themselves in his face when he was alive had smoothed out, and his hair, lackluster at best, before he collapsed in front of the library clutching his chest, had regained some body and even some color. There wasn't any green decomposing skin, no withered lips and rotted gums, nothing like that. Is this what zombies really look like? Wait, are zombies real and this is what happens? I had convinced myself that I was halluci-nating somewhere along the way and was settling into the fantasy... and it was freaking me out fast. Do we just reani-mate after we die and go on about our merry way? Shouldn't you move to a new town if you're going to do that? I mean, what if you bump into someone that knew you when you were alive -.

It was the wave that did me in.

Just a gentle flick of the wrist: an open-handed salute. It was so jovial, so natural. His hand seemed to glow. The sky behind him was the brightest, darkest blue I'd ever seen. It was like the night sky was backlit by a spotlight or some-thing. It made the sky weird. Too blue. It was kind of like the color of the water you see when you're out in the middle of the ocean. That's how it looked on that cruise Mom and Dad took me on before I started high school. The water was so deep out there – it seemed like you would never find the bottom if you dropped anchor. I remember staring at it every day, getting more and more spooked. How could anyone survive out there? Who knows what lurks beneath the surface?

Blue, teal, turquoise, and midnight all rolled into one - that's what the color of the sky looked like. It was as wrong as Mr. Ridley was. His hand looked obscenely bright against it, but he didn't seem to notice. He just went on waving at me under the weirdest-looking sky I'd ever seen.

Please don't smile.

I don't think I can handle it if he smiles.

I didn't feel my car careen off the road and hit the turn-buckle because I was too busy staring at Mr. Ridley and the sky. The sky and Mr. Ridley. I passed out before the impact, praying that Mr. Ridley didn't smile and show me his pointy teeth.

4

I didn't know I was looking for something new, but damn, he is gorgeous. Dirty blond, blue eyes, with abs that lead into the most perfect pelvic muscle I've ever seen up close. Australian accent on a velvety voice, barely legal, and eager. He's the polar opposite of any other man I've ever been with, but I'm not complaining. He takes his time and savors me like fine wine. I could listen to him moan all day long, and sometimes I do just that. He leaves me satisfied and crazy for more.

I'm so preoccupied with Dustin that I rarely even think of Jared anymore.

Dustin adores me. He says as much, but that's not how I know. It's when I catch him looking at me out of the corner of my eye that speaks volumes. His face goes through so many emotions at once, it's almost painful to watch. Love, admiration, obsession, lust. Fear. He wants this to last forever and doesn't know if it can.

He's beautiful and smart.

He loves the sun and lets it kiss his skin with zeal; watching him take off his shirt in its yellow glow is an exercise in restraint. He wants to marry me, but that will never be. Regardless of what happens between Jared and I, I would never go on record as being 21 years my husband's senior. Dustin just laughs when I say that. He says he'll push my wheelchair out to see the surf every day if that's what I want. Ah, my pretty. I think he really believes he would.

He met me on the beach today. Just ran by me with his board under his arm; I sensed him more than saw him until he had run several paces away. He threw a kiss over his shoulder and dove into the tumultuous sea, ready to enjoy the waves for as long as the sunlight held. I was content to watch him move in the water, read my book, and feel the breeze.

This had become my typical day, and I loved every minute of it.

Sometimes I wondered what was going on between us. Is this just a fling? How did this happen? There are so many things that I don't remember. I feel like I'm drunk on whatever this is – passion, lust, love? I don't remember when I decided I was going to cheat on Jared. We weren't having any problems – life was the comfortable normal that marriages slip into over time. I know Jared as well as I know myself – does he know what I've been up to?

As I watched Dustin come out of the surf, I can understand what caught my eye. Any woman would be hard pressed to not do a double take. But I never thought I'd cheat.

As Dustin came closer, those thoughts were invaded by others – ones that make me shift in my seat. It made the worries seem unimportant. For now.

I felt my cheeks get hot as he stood over me. His lopsided smile was my undoing. I felt flutters deep in my belly and had to look away. This is one hell of a forty-something-woman-going-through-a-midlife-crisis checklist item, that's for sure.

Dustin laid me down on the sand. He kissed my eyelids, my cheekbones, my nose, my mouth. His touch, made rough by the white sand, still managed to raise goose bumps on my skin. He stretched my arms overhead, clasped one hand in his, palm to palm, fingers interlaced like first loves often do, and traced a line from my elbow to waist with the other, watching his fingers as they moved. I could see the desire in his eyes as he looked at my body, could sense the control he struggled to keep over himself. He bit his lip to keep it at bay, his desire threatening to quicken his pace. He wanted to go slowly because he knew I liked it when he did, even though he felt like he couldn't wait any longer. He wanted to savor me, though his mouth watered. That realization affected me in a way I didn't expect. The tears that stung the corners of my eyes were real. Exhilaratingly real, and so very scary.

He guided himself inside me without ever letting go of my hand.

The sky looked incredible. Such a brilliant blue. I was

trying to come up with the name for it; the name was just on the tip of my tongue when Dustin sent me over the edge. Then I started thinking about how I might never go home if this pretty young thing plans to fuck me like this every time.

And then I stopped thinking altogether.

The last thing I saw before I woke up to the brilliant blue of that weird sky was the first thing I was looking for but couldn't find. Where is Dustin? I looked around, taking in all the people scattered about in various stages of confusion, but none of them kept my attention. But the sky did. It kept pulling my eyes away from the task. Though the color was the same, it wasn't beautiful to me anymore. It was all-encompassing and thick. Heavy. It seemed to bear down on me, as interested in crushing me as hovering above me. I felt its menace in every part of my body.

My clothes were the same, just a sundress and sandals, still hiked up over my hips the way Dustin had me. My skin looked the same, and I felt the same. But everything had changed.

"Dustin?"

I whispered his name at first, not wanting to draw the attention of the others, though that might have been impossible, anyway.

I was lying in a tree that was close to the ground. It was very much like the Divi Divi trees that grow in Aruba with their affected lean and gnarled roots. My toes scraped the ground from my perch, but the rest of my body was enclosed in the tree as though I was sitting in its mouth. And the leaves were so green. Breathtakingly green. The most intensely bright green I had ever seen before. The tree, the whole place, was alive in a way that nature wasn't intended to be. I felt like a cricket veering too close to a Venus flytrap.

I pried myself out of the tree's grip and stood on grass that crunched underfoot. "Dustin?" I said again, panic invading my voice. He shouldn't be here – I know that now. More than anything, I hoped he wasn't here. That sweet man, who loved me right when I needed it, shouldn't have to endure this. I didn't want to know what his face looked like in the light of the harsh crayon sun that hung overhead like a weight.

It dawned on me that this is exactly where I belonged. It felt like some kind of reverse Rapture. All the good people stayed on Earth, and the bad ones – the ones who cheated and didn't think twice about their husbands - were sent to hell. Because this is hell, right?

It certainly feels like it.

I saw him approaching in the distance and wondered about his size. Jared was a big man, sure, but something about him seemed disproportionate somehow. And his gait– it was too deliberate. Almost like he was trying too hard to put one foot in front of the other. I shook my head in resignation. This is what I deserve, isn't it? Not Dustin, but Jared – new and improved... and sure to be mad as hell. I bought it and paid for it, indeed.

"Corinne, baby! Oh, thank God!"

The words were his, but the voice wasn't. But that's all right. As Jared's arms encircled me, pulling me into his soft, fleshy chest, the name of that color blue popped into my mind. Cerulean. That's what it was. The color of the Caribbean Sea transposed in the sky. My eyes fell on the faces of people I don't know. Some of them were paralyzed with fear and others in blissful ignorance of what lay ahead. I'm too sad to be scared even though Jared's embrace felt more like a vise.

5

Hazy.

That's what it seemed like, but not what it was.

Maybe my vision was hazy - maybe my mind. I wanted to go back to sleep. But I hadn't been sleeping, had I?

Not really.

Wishing for it, maybe. Sleep was all I wanted to do these days. Being awake was a chore; the constant hemming and hawing about trivial things that most people my age engaged in had started to grate on my nerves a long time ago. I wanted to shut all of that nonsense out. I did everything I could to make it go away, short of the final step.

Is that what this was? Had I finally gotten rid of that Catholic guilt and found the balls to do what needed to be done? Caroline would be disappointed to see me this way, if seeing the dead again is what really happens when all is said and done. She might say, in that exasperated tone she reserved just for me, Oh, Edward,' and give me a good smack to prove that point. But I would take it if it meant being with her again. I'd give anything to hear the sound of her voice again.

What took me so long to do it? When Caroline died all those years ago, I thought I would go after her. I was sick. Hell, I had been sick first, so it made sense. But then my heart disease got under control (the doctors kept referring to my cluster of heart attacks as blips on my screen) and my health rebounded – not all the way, but enough to keep me kicking. The doctors patted each other on the back; the kids cheered and hugged, but I sulked. I pulled away, stayed home more because that's where it was quiet. I stopped seeing the doctor because I wanted whatever they did to be undone. I wanted to go with Caroline. Life without her wasn't much of a life at all.

But that was eight years ago. Eight years of living in the shadows, watching trash TV, crying over old pictures, only speaking to the kids when they pressed the issue: avoiding life. They knew what was going on – Robbie said he'd help me do it if I really wanted to. But I couldn't saddle him with that for the rest of his life. My good boy would suffer too, and I didn't want that to happen.

I learned something over those eight years. You can't will death. It'll come when it's good and ready and not a moment before.

I remember going to bed with Caroline and the kids on my mind. I was thinking about an outing at the lake up in Greenbrier, MD, from 40 years ago. The sun was shining, and a cool breeze ruffled my hair. I could feel warmth on my cheeks even in the darkness of the one room I lived out of anymore. I couldn't make myself walk around the house much. Too many ghosts occupy the rooms.

I don't remember deciding to do it. I had contemplated the ways a million times – pills seemed the easiest. The thought of shooting myself and not dying made me sick to my stomach. I didn't think I could take a knife to myself, and I wasn't about to jump off anything. Pills I could do. I'd just take all the doses of Tambocor that I missed and let my heart literally skip a beat. It would be quick. Not painless, but that's not what I'm looking for.

But then this happened.

I looked around at the landscape I woke up to. It was beautiful, yet odd in a way that frightened me. My house was gone. In fact, I couldn't see any houses at all. There were too many people around - people who were paying attention to everyone else but trying to look like they weren't. And the sky. There was something wrong with the sky. It was like a kid's coloring page – the colors were too bright and unrealistic. And harsh.

Where the hell is Caroline?

If this is what I think it is and I've checked out of life once and for all, why isn't she here to greet me? She can't still be mad that I put her in a home, not after all these years... could she?

Some people were crying quietly. Some cried out loud with such gut-wrenching wails they made my hair stand on end. Some got angry, demanding an answer, a reason for being in this new place – they stood shouting into the open air. Others hugged themselves against the outside world. Me, I just sat and watched. I didn't think I had enough control over myself to do anything else.

6

The room was alive for the first time since the beginning, buzzing and beeping accompanied by loud, fast-talking nurses and doctors. There was a lot of reaching, running, and commotion. And then nothing. No movement, no people, no noise.

Dr. Mitchell stood in the middle of the room, his vantage point allowing a view of all of them. Jennifer, 28. Brandon, 33. Carrie, 19. Corinne, 41. Edward, 77. All wheeled into the large room that would end up being their death chamber within minutes of each other. All gone at virtually the same time.

The hallucinogen had been injected into each patients IV in tandem. Brain scans for each of them showed hyperactivity spikes and relaxed rhythms at the same pace. They seemed to enter the new sphere, a place designed to comfort them as they awaited their deaths, at the same time also. Cerulean Fields was his life's work: a utopia for the dying. It was supposed to give them peace at the end instead of pain, a loss of dignity, and fear.

But it didn't. It couldn't have. In the end, they were all writhing, fighting, clawing at the air. Something chased them to their deaths over there. Something unexpected.

He looked at the pictures of his patients that were posted on their bedside tables and felt a sadness well in him that he had dreaded from the beginning of the research. He had never met them; by the time they arrived at the facility, their induced comas had already taken effect. He didn't want to know them, didn't want to see their eyes. That would have just complicated things.

The pictures showed each of his patients in the prime of their lives, their smiling faces a testament to their health in contrast to their present situation. Edward stood tall and confident, muscular in the way that men who enjoyed the outdoors were. His son Robert said that Edward had been an avid camper, taking the kids into the woods every summer. Robert couldn't bear to see his father like this, so frail and thin. It took everything he had to visit every week.

Jennifer's picture didn't look like her at all – the stroke paralyzed her entire left side and aged her overnight. Brandon's picture was of him out at a lake. You could only see his profile, but that's the only image that his girlfriend would bring. She only came to visit once and didn't stay long. Carrie's picture was haunting. It showed a sweet little high school kid with her whole life ahead of her. It was Carrie before the drugs and the self-imposed isolation. It was Carrie before the accident.

Corinne was the true beauty in the bunch. Dr. Mitchell's affinity for her was evident from the start. He could see a beautiful woman beneath the graying skin. Looking at her grounded him; made him see the patients as people instead of research specimens. Every time he looked at the picture of her on the beach with her sarong flowing in the wind, revealing slender, shapely legs, he grew more attached. Her caramel skin, sun-kissed in the picture, seemed to glow. She radiated confidence even before the vast sea in front of her.

He wished he knew her before the cancer ravaged her body, before chemotherapy stole her hair, before her eyes closed forever. If they had met in a coffee shop, would she have noticed him? Would she order a Chai tea latte and turn to see him staring at her? Would she smile the same way she did in the picture, joyful and provocative, and make his knees buckle? If they met on a crowded street, would she be interested in him, or would his blue eyes not be her cup of tea? Sometimes he got angry because he would never have the chance to find out.

Sometimes he touched Corinne's hand when he thought of what could have been, wanting to feel her skin next to his own. He interlaced their fingers when the fantasy was particularly compelling, gingerly holding her paper-thin skin against his, gaining closer contact in the most appropriate way possible even though, in his mind, they moved from hugging to kissing to more. He imagined how he would caress her skin, run his hands through her hair, kiss her beautiful full lips - lips that had only been parted to brace a feeding tube since he had known her. Dr. Mitchell spoke to her about the places they would have gone if they had the chance, sharing a fantasy that could never come true with a woman he wasn't entirely sure could hear him. He felt like a kid talking about his hopes and dreams. Corinne made him giddy in a way that he hadn't been since he was 20 years old. He regaled in a past they never shared and mourned a future that would never be. Many times, he wondered how life could be so cruel to show him true love in the touch of a dying woman.

Dr. Mitchell looked at Corrine, studied her. This would be the last time he saw her. Once he left the room she shared with the other patients, their connection would be lost. He was not ready to say goodbye.

He puttered around the room a bit more, cleaning up, wasting time, trying to prepare himself for the inevitable. Soon the families would be notified, and the bodies would be claimed. They would be gone within hours. Corrine would be gone forever.

The thought was unbearable.

"Dr. Mitchell, we need your signature on the files."

The nurse's voice barely registered to him. The only sound he could hear was waves crashing on the shore.

"Dustin?"

The nurse had moved close enough to touch his arm. He had to restrain himself from shaking her hand off. She handed him the folders and left him alone. He saw the concern in her eyes as she did, but she was mercifully silent.

He touched Corinne's hand one last time. It was still warm. Perhaps that was the worst part.

\/\\|/\\|/

THE BLACK HOLE

1

"Damn, man, gotta bring a nigga out to the boonies to play souped-up tag," Shaun said in his best thug impersonation as he looked through the fogged window of Martin's black Cherokee Limited Edition. It was cold that morning, and he could see his breath in the air when he rolled down the window to get a better look outside.

"Shaun, what's up with the window? It's not like it's summer up in here," Martin said.

Shaun was too busy making faces and hand gestures at Gary, Kevin, and Robert in the forest green Jetta following behind them to pay attention to what Martin was saying. He was pointing out the horses grazing in the field on the right side of the car and shaking his head.

"Are you sure we're going the right way, Martin? I don't see any street signs," Craig asked as he looked curiously at the bales of hay neatly stacked on the driven land to the left of the car. He poked Shaun and said,

"Are you seeing this shit? It's like we drove out of Maryland and into the backwoods of North Carolina!"

"I've followed the directions to the letter. They told me there wouldn't be any street signs. Nothing but farmland in sight for miles, they said," Martin picked up the crumpled piece of paper that had the directions on it and double-checked his steps. He had been invited to play 'Capture the Flag' by a guy he worked with. It was a dare, really. Martin heard about the paintball craze before. A lot of the kids in his area seemed to like to do it on Friday nights with flashlights on their face masks. They would go into the woods and shoot at each other like crazy until one of the teams surrendered. It was nothing but a little fad that the kids would soon be tired of, he thought. Nothing but a fad.

His co-worker, Jeremy, issued the paintball challenge to him one day during lunch. He said that he and a couple of his buddies go out every once in a while, and horse around after work to shake the stress off. He said it was a lot of fun and a damned good release. *'Lord knows I could use that,'* Martin thought while Jeremy explained the rules to him. What Jeremy told him seemed to be a lot different from what he had heard before about paintball. He thought that playing paintball, or going paintballing, or whatever you called it, was nothing more than a kid's game. It certainly wasn't anything that he and his boys would want to do with their Saturday afternoons. Hoops was more like their speed - not pseudo-military combat with pretty little pink paintballs that splatter all over you on impact and color your clothes with water-solvent fluorescent paint. No, a real challenge was to take it to the hoop and slam it down somebody's throat.

That's a game. That's sport. That's relaxing. It's what he and his boys did to shake the stress off.

Martin tried to explain the differences, both physical and mental, to Jeremy at lunch. For every point he brought up, Jeremy countered with another. It went on for almost the entire hour, both of their sandwiches going completely untouched. Finally, he said it. Jeremy issued the challenge.

"You want to try it? Your men against mine in the brush? I mean, that's if you can handle it," Jeremy said with a taunting smirk on his face. He sat back dramatically in his chair, satisfied with his lead. Jack, the controller, who was sitting at another table, inched forward on Martin's pause. His forehead was peppered with sweat, and his skin was furrowed with anticipation. Martin glanced over at Jack, and he looked away quickly, trying to act nonchalant. He began eating his sandwich slowly, his eyes darting towards Martin's table. Martin shook his head in amusement and turned back to Jeremy. Jack looked up from his sandwich and turned his attention to Jeremy and Martin's conversation again. He was listening, eagerly awaiting Martin's response. Martin was amazed at Jack's intrusion and tried to ignore it as he said,

"You don't think I'll play, do you?"

Jeremy shrugged his shoulders theatrically.

"Would you come out to the court and sweat it up with the big boys?" Martin asked. He didn't think that Jeremy would bring his lily-white, country-club friends down to the gym to play b-ball with a bunch of Black guys. Not that he and his boys played ball in Southeast, DC, but anywhere in Chocolate City would scare the pants off the likes of Jeremy and his boys. It's a wonder Jeremy made it to work in Northwest without hyperventilating in his car.

Martin had met some of Jeremy's friends before. One

day after work, he and Jeremy met up with them in George-town for happy hour. They were in some hoity-toity bar where the drinks were extremely expensive and watered down. Places like that were always full of loose girls who were willing and able if you bought them enough drinks and patted them on the ass real nice. They flaunted their plastic surgeon's sculptured breasts in increments, teasing you with what could happen later, as long as the car you had parked outside was a BMW or a Porsche. Yeah, it was that kind of place.

Jeremy's friends Kurt, Chuck, and Brad came to the bar fifteen minutes after Martin and Jeremy arrived. Jeremy and his friends graduated from Georgetown University. Martin came out of Howard University. Even with four against one odds, a pretty heated discussion ensued about the two alma maters. They bickered over curriculum, campus structure, student government, etcetera, but the real conversation (the underlying jab) was about the competence of historically black universities versus white universities.

Kevin, Martin's friend and fellow alumni met up with them about an hour into the discussion. He sat down and loosened his tie, listening to the back and forth, and shook his head. It was the same ole thing. It seemed that every time he and Martin went out with White boys, they always wanted to talk about who is better. Inadvertently and undercover, for sure. But it was always the same discussion. Don't they ever get tired of it?

While he sipped a Kahlua and Cream, the old white magic went to work. His friends called it white magic because Kevin had a knack for picking up women without even trying to. White women. He was like a magnet. They flocked to him like he was the best thing since hotcakes. The first one that came over was blonde. She was tall and slender, with breasts as big and round as the water balloons that kids used to throw off the roof to hit the mailman. Martin had a fleeting daydream about touching them. He wondered if they would pop if he squeezed too hard. He chuckled at the mental image and caught a glimpse of Jeremy and his friends. Jeremy was looking distractedly around the table and the bar. It was so deliberate, the way he looked past Kevin and the girl. He looked as if he wished that no one could see him sitting there. He creatively dodged the courting going on in front of him (if that's what you called it) by pretending to be intensely interested in the busy crowd funneling into the tiny bar. He watched as men checked women out and women coyly lured men in with no interest. He just needed something to avert his eyes from the scene unraveling before him. Brad had a sour look on his face. He kept staring at the girl, trying desperately to make eye contact. Chuck looked like he was going to be sick. His skin had taken on a strange green tone, and his eyes were watery. The murmur of the crowd around them seemed far away.

Martin looked at Kevin and his lady de jour. He was working it, throwing every line he could at her. She was sitting on the stool closest to him. So close she could probably feel his breath on her face. She was fine. Martin was sure that's why Jeremy and his friends were reacting the way they were. Jealousy, pure and simple. He applauded Kevin inside.

Kevin got the girl's number and kissed her lightly before she left. When she walked away, he shot Martin a look that said, 'No sweat, man. It's as easy as pie.' Martin shook his head and laughed as he patted him on the back. That was his boy. Martin never had a problem getting girls, either. He had been told time and time again that his soft hazel brown eyes were capable of hypnotizing women. That's what they said after the fact. Martin hadn't figured out the trick to make women come after *him*. Sure, he could close the deal when he went to them, but they hardly ever made that uncertain, 'everyone's looking at me' walk across a crowded room to go and talk to him like they did for Kevin. None of them. Black, White, Asian, Spanish, Indian, none of them. Not for Martin.

Kevin had to work at getting play with his own, though. Black women were used to his chocolate brown skin being silky-smooth. They were used to his naturally curly hair having a little wave to it. Black women didn't bug out on that kind of stuff. It didn't float them as easily as it floated White women. White women just loved Kevin's 'deep' skin. It was enough to make a light-skinned brother like Martin mad. Not that he wanted attention from White women so much; he was quite content with his Black Queens. But it was an ego thing. Play seemed to fall into Kevin's lap, and Martin had to work for him. That kind of thing messes with a man's head.

The six of them started talking again. The conversation seemed so normal, and everyone seemed to be having such a good time that Martin shook off what he thought he saw when Kevin was talking to the woman. Not ten minutes after the blonde-haired woman left did a brown-haired woman stare in Kevin's direction. He saw her and motioned for her to come over to the table. White magic. Kevin was player-elite again. Just like that.

As Kevin turned his back to the guys, Martin got ready to comment on his 'flow' in jest. But he didn't. When he looked at Jeremy and his friends, their expressions were indescribable. There was an evil look mirrored on all four of their faces. Mutual disgust. It was only there for a second, just one split second, but Martin saw it. He saw it, and it made him uneasy. It made him angry. That was the last time they all hung out.

But there, in the lunch area at work, Martin couldn't ignore the challenge. Even though he didn't particularly care for Jeremy and his friends, he couldn't make himself pass it up. He knew that he and his boys could beat any bunch of White men at any sport, except maybe hockey. He knew that like he knew his own name. He relished the idea of being able to beat Jeremy and his boys at their own game. Martin wanted to beat them for the look they gave Kevin at the bar (or at least, the look he *thought* they gave Kevin. He never told anyone about that because he wasn't one hundred percent sure he saw it. He had been drinking, after all.), and what that look really meant.

Martin got himself so riled up that he fantasized about the game. The night before the event, Martin, Kevin, Shaun, Gary, Craig, and Robert went out for drinks. After about three beers and a lot of trash talking, Martin slipped into an alcohol-induced daydream. He envisioned a plantation on which he and his friends were slaves. They had been taken from Africa to work for Jeremy and his kind. Martin imagined a great uprising where he and his friends broke their shackles and ran for the woods, determined to gain their freedom. The slave owners, led by Jeremy, advanced upon them with fire lighting their way, but he and his friends fought them off and made them retreat. Chuckling himself back to reality, Martin raised his fourth beer in a toast and said,

"Let's show Jeremy and his boys who's runnin' shit up in here. Paintball, basketball, baseball, racquetball, any kind of ball game they want. There's no stoppin' us."

They all raised their bottles and toasted the declaration. They were ready for paintball.

That was the last time they drank together.

2

"Man, I don't think we're going the right way," Shaun muttered as they passed through the farmland. It was a gray and cool day. Something about how the sky looked bothered him. He wasn't up for this, not like the others were. He glanced warily out of the window.

"Look, Martin. There's a sign." Craig pointed at a little cardstock sign flopping around on its stick. It was colored with what must have been fluorescent paint a long time ago. Now it just looked like faded orange and yellow.

'Pete's Paintball.

Play with a group.

Next Left.'

"I'm guessing that's it," Craig said playfully.

"No shit, Sherlock," Martin retorted. He made a left turn onto a makeshift driveway. There had been a lot of rain in the area over the past couple of days, and the land was nothing but a muddy mess. Martin drove slowly, being careful not to get stuck. He didn't know how far the paintball field was from where they were, which was out in the middle of nowhere. It was certainly not the right time to get stuck, if there ever was a right time. Gary pulled off the driveway and onto the grass. The Jetta couldn't handle the mud. Martin decided to do the

same, and he followed Gary up a winding driveway that led onto a private street.

In the overcast lighting of the Saturday morning, the tree-lined street looked ominous. There were towering oaks and maple trees growing haphazardly in the thick of the woods. The leaves had been falling for the past couple of weeks, and the ground was covered with what looked like two inches of red and orange foliage. Evergreens and Cedar trees stood tall and thick. They were sinister-looking on that cold November day. The trees were unyielding. Their appearance was upstaged by the leafless, contorted branches of the Dogwood and Magnolia trees that lurked in the thick. They deflected one's sight from the Pine trees and the tangled brush. The trunks looked like horribly distorted torsos in the light of that overcast day. They likened themselves to a visual of tortured souls. The branches seemed to be reaching towards the cars, trying to suck them into the thick underbrush that lay below their massive bases. Shaun recoiled in his seat at the sight of them.

"Y'all ready to kick some ass?" Martin shouted in the truck. He was trying to rile them up; trying to get them motivated for the excursion. He too, felt a little funny about the woods they were driving deeper into. He didn't like the sight of it one bit. But what the hell? It was just a stupid paintball game for kids. Right?

"Yeah, man. Yeah! I can feel the gun in my hands already." Craig held an imaginary gun in the shape of a rifle and aimed out of the window. With one eye squeezed shut, he cocked it and shot. He looked out at the trees. It seemed like the leaves rustled just as he shot the fake plug into the woods. He shivered unconsciously.

3

He saw a Cherokee and a Jetta make the turn onto the road leading to the paintball site through his binoculars. He zoomed in and saw one of the boys in the car looking around his woods nervously. He chuckled to himself. 'Be nervous, boy. Should be. Ain't got no kinda idea what you got comin' do ya? Soon enough, though. Soon enough,' the old man said to the empty room and let out a cackling laugh that shook his entire body. He put down the binoculars and called to his son.

4

Martin jumped out of the truck onto the moist, leaf-covered ground and looked around slowly. He tossed his keys back to Craig, like usual. Martin had been prone to losing his keys. Since he was eighteen or so he had passed his keys to Craig for safekeeping. Craig picked on him when he did it. He would make a big deal about it, laughing and calling him absent-minded. This time he didn't say a word.

It was quiet. He could hear the leaves crunching under his feet as he walked. Tall, threatening trees stood around them, encasing them in a wooden heaven... or hell. Shaun was the first one to break the silence.

"I don't think I've ever been out in woods like these. I mean, my grandmother's house has a little patch of trees in the back, but nothing like this. It's so..."

"Dark," Gary cut in. He put the steering wheel lock on

his Jetta out of habit and got out of the car. His face looked concerned; worried. So did Kevin's.

"Hey y'all! C'mon back this way. The paintball field is way in the back, down here." A short man came out from behind the bushes and called out to them. It was like he came out of nowhere. He was wearing dingy overalls and an old baseball cap that had seen better days. With a grin, he motioned for them to follow him deeper into the woods on foot. Martin went first. He thought that if he didn't, no one would. As he followed the old man and heard his friends falling in behind him, he thought about the last five minutes. They got out of the car in what seemed like a barren patch of land in the woods. There was no sound. There was no movement other than their own. Suddenly, there was a guy talking at them. Giddy like. It looked as though he was excited to see them. Exceedingly excited. Something was wrong with that. Martin was uneasy, but he didn't want to let his friends know that. They already seemed a little apprehensive about the situation. He walked behind the old man with caution.

They went down a steep hill that led deeper into the woods. Robert looked back and couldn't see the car. He whispered to Martin.

"I can't even see the car anymore. We're really going deep in here, huh?"

"Good," Martin said without turning around, "this way we won't hit the cars with any paint. You know I'd be pissed off if I messed up my truck."

He chuckled and picked up the pace behind the man. Robert looked back towards the car and shook his head, disturbed.

The man stopped in front of a dilapidated wooden shed and said,

"Right here's where y'all will meet up wit' the other team. Go'n be a good game today, yup. I'ma go an' get 'em right now. Y'all stay put." He walked around the corner and disappeared as quickly as he had appeared by the cars. They looked at each other in silence. Kevin said,

"So, what do we do now?" Gary asked.

"I guess we wait. Jeremy will be here soon enough," Martin said. After about 15 minutes, Martin saw them coming down the hill, eight strong. They were dressed in fatigues and seemed in unison with their stride. Looking at them was like watching a platoon prepare for battle. They were focused and serious. Martin's stomach dropped.

Jeremy was ahead of the pack. He looked confident and determined. He walked up to Martin and said with a straight face,

"I'm really glad you came. You and your...friends."

He glanced through them, committing their innuendos to memory. He looked back at Martin with soft venom in his eyes. Martin saw the change in Jeremy, but only for a second. He wasn't sure what it meant, but he didn't like it. He was starting not to like much about the setup for this game.

Jeremy's face lightened, and he offered a chuckle, but his eyes remained cold. He said, "You remember Chuck, Kurt, and Brad, don't you? Eddie, Doug, Wally, and Steve came along too. This should be a real good game."

"You've met Kevin. This is Shaun, Gary, Craig, and Robert." Martin pointed them out one by one to Jeremy and his friends. It was a stare down, but no one acknowledged it as such. It became clear to Martin that they weren't there just to play tag in the woods.

"Looks like we've got two more guys than you do. Tell you what, why don't we even it up? Make it seven on seven.

Take your pick of one of our men," Jeremy said to Martin. He was smiling, but there was no warmth coming from it. He was cold. There was something glistening maliciously in his eyes. Hate, fear, jealousy - Martin wasn't sure. But he saw it... again. And Jeremy knew it.

Martin looked at the guys Jeremy brought with him. They were all of average build, nothing spectacular. *'Nothing me and my boys can't handle,'* the little voice in his head chimed in. They all had a certain confidence about them. Not inherent, he didn't think. No, it was more like they had set something up, some prime situation that they had complete control over. They were ready to play. They were sure to win. He glanced tentatively at his friends. They were all strong, all athletic. Physically, Jeremy and his friends were no match for them. But something in the back of his mind told him that this was not going to be a challenge of will and stamina. This would be something worse than that... something much more important than that.

Craig spoke up and said, "OK, since we get to pick. How about you?"

Craig pointed at Chuck. He was the bulkiest guy on Jeremy's team. He looked like he worked out more than the others, and that would make him able to handle the challenge ahead. He thought.

"What's your name, partner?"

"Chuck," he said as he snickered and looked back at his friends. He walked towards Martin's team and said, "Sure, I'm game."

"Looks like we've got a game, then! Let's head up so we can get this started." Jeremy announced as he led the way to the ammo station. They followed in single file, silently, contemplating the situation. Shaun looked over at Martin as if to ask a question, but shook his head instead. Martin shrugged and slapped Shaun on the back in an effort to reassure him that things were cool. It was just a game, after all. Shaun looked away, his face grimacing slightly with worry.

5

Both teams got their ammo and bought extra just in case they ran out in the heat of battle. While they loaded their guns, Martin and his team had a strategy huddle. "We have to be ready for them to come out of a bag on us. Jeremy knows this is our first time playing. We're not going to let them take us though, right?" he questioned.

"Naw, man, no. This'll be a piece of cake. We just have to stick to the plan. Get the flag and cover each other," Kevin offered.

"We should make sure that we have one person at the fort protecting the flag at all times, just in case they infiltrate somehow," Chuck added.

"Yeah, yeah. I don't know about you, but I want to be out in the middle of things. I want to go for the flag and bring it home," Robert said uncharacteristically. Robert was usually the one who waited for other people to take control of things before he jumped in. He'd been that way for as long as Martin had known him, and that was about 10 years. In high school, he wouldn't go out for basketball unless at least one of his boys was going out for it too. He wouldn't go to a party unless one of his boys was going, even when a girl asked him to go. He even went to Howard University because Martin and Kevin were going. So when he stepped up to the plate, wanting to be the one to go for the flag, everyone looked at him in shock.

Robert looked at their surprised eyes and said, "What? A brother can't want his 15 minutes of fame? Step off, y'all."

They laughed as he rolled his eyes. Shaun looked over at the other group while his laughter subsided. They weren't in a huddle like his team was, strategizing and planning. They weren't talking to each other at all. Jeremy and his team were staring at them. One of them was looking right into his eyes. Shaun looked back, unwilling to tear his eyes away. Unwilling or unable. Everything else became dark around him. Tunnel vision blocked everyone else out. The shirt the guy was wearing was completely out of focus, and the features of his face were blurry. The only things Shaun could see clearly were his eyes. They were a light shade of green, but to Shaun, they looked as black as ebony. Dark and small. They were so hot they could bore holes into his head, he thought. He looked away to shake himself from the grip.

"You okay, man?" Craig asked him. He looked like he had just seen a ghost. Craig looked in the direction that Shaun had been staring towards and saw nothing out of the ordinary. Just the other team going over their plans, just like they had been doing. He put his hand on Shaun's back and said, "Man, what's the deal?"

"I don't know, I thought I saw something. I thought-" He stopped short and looked at Chuck. He was staring at him with dark eyes...for one second. When he blinked, Chuck looked normal. He looked like a regular guy, concerned for his teammate. Not like a ghoul or a man with something up his sleeve. Just a regular guy.

"Nothing. I'm cool. I'm cool," Shaun said. He glanced

tentatively back at Chuck, who still looked ...normal. A shiver crept up his spine.

"OK, since Robert's layin' down the law, we go with that plan," Kevin continued. "Me and Rob'll go up the middle for the flag; we'll need two to stay with our flag and everyone else needs to disperse and take care of things as they come. Plan?"

"Yeah, that'll work," Shaun offered. He sounded more like he was trying to convince himself than just agreeing with the plan.

They broke the huddle and prepared for the referee's word. A beefy man dressed in fatigues with a fluorescent orange pullover vest stretched tightly across his torso stood between the two teams. Martin looked at him and nodded hello. The man returned a smirk and glanced over at Jeremy's team with a knowing glance. Confused, Martin looked at Kevin, who was standing next to him, and said, "Did you see that, Ref? What's up with that?"

"I don't know, man," he said as he looked at Jeremy and his friends. They were ready. Mentally and physically. They had all the extras as well. They had smoke bombs, sidearms, grenades, you name it. He didn't even know they made those kinds of accessories for paintball. Something about that made him nervous. Martin shook his head lightly. "Don't sweat it," he finished.

The referee spoke loudly into the bullhorn. In a muffled voice he yelled, "The idea is to get the flag and take it to your fort. If you get hit three times, you out the game fer good. Do y'all get that? The game is over when one team has took the other team's flag, or when there's only one man standing. Got that? Play to the end, boys. This is war." He held up two bandannas – one yellow and one red. "These is yo' flags.

Jeremy's boys got the yellow one, and you boys got the red one." He tossed the flag lackadaisically to Martin. "If there ain't no questions, I say let's get this goin'. Any questions?" No one said anything.

"When I blow this whistle, it means y'all got 'bout one minute to get to yo' places. When I blow it again, the game starts. Here she goes."

He licked the perspiration off his upper lip and blew the whistle. The two teams dispersed, hanging their flags in equidistant forts on low branches, and securing their hiding places. They moved without a sound. Martin and Shaun were protecting the flag; Robert and Kevin were the flag runners going up the middle on opposite sides of the path, and Craig, Chuck and Gary were on the outskirts protecting the flag runners like linebackers.

When Kevin got to his hiding place, he could hear Shaun behind him breathing heavily.

"What is it, man? You ok?"

"Yeah man. I-I'm fine," Shaun responded. But he was far from fine.

The whistle sounded for the second time.

The game had begun.

6

They sat in complete silence for an eternity. Their hearts beat loudly and rapidly in their chests. Martin looked between the bushes at his friends. They were tense and uptight. There was something brewing in the woods that was more than competitiveness. It was more like fear. Genuine, uncontested fear. And they all felt it. Even him.

Kevin knelt hidden in the brush, covered by leaves and twigs as camouflage. Beads of sweat fell into his eyes underneath the protective goggles, stinging them, but he dared not wipe his forehead. He didn't want to move at all. Something was going on, and he knew it. *'Something is wrong with this setup,'* he thought. *'I mean, those guys came down looking serious about...something.'* This wasn't just an ordinary game of paintball. He knew it the moment he saw the other team. He could tell by the way Jeremy and his friends were looking at them. Jeremy and his friends were looking at them like they were fresh meat, a succulent cut at that. It made him nervous.

He looked beyond the tree at Jeremy's fort. He could barely see their flag above the bushes and tall grass. He couldn't see any of Jeremy's team either. Not one person. He adjusted his footing and raised up slightly to get a better look. He thought he saw movement, so he shot off a round of pink paint. The paintball shot out of the gun, propelled by the CO_2 tank connected to its base, and splattered against a tree. When there was no retaliation, Kevin relaxed back into his hiding place. He didn't see the gunman in the bushes picking him out. He didn't hear the barrel cock as the gunman took aim. He didn't see the barrel squared off at his head. He didn't hear the bullet cut the air. He didn't see or hear anything at all.

7

"Did you hear that?" Shaun shrieked in a low, raspy, panicked voice. They all hit the dirt as soon as the pop of the

bullet broke the uncomfortable silence. "It sounded like gunfire. Real gunfire, man! What the fuck is going on?"

Martin was crouched in the thick of kikuyugrass, his eyes searching frantically. The shot rang in his ears loudly, incessantly. He looked nervously around for his friends. Robert was standing now, looking around himself in fear. Martin wanted to yell out to Robert and tell him to sit down, to take cover, to run, damnit, but when he opened his mouth, nothing came out. Nothing. He tried to inch towards Shaun, who was across the weathered path from him, lying in a makeshift bunker. He wanted to go to him so that he wouldn't be alone. So that neither one of them would be alone... but he couldn't move.

A second shot was fired, and a gargled scream permeated the air thick with tension and fear. Martin looked up just in time to see Robert grab at his throat. Blood shot out in spurts between his fingers, mimicking his racing heartbeat. Robert gagged and coughed, trying desperately to catch his breath. His bulging eyes were glazed over with pain. He fell to his knees and sprayed the mallow with his dying blood.

'Oh Shit! Oh, Holy shit,' Martin thought to himself. He peered over the tangleweed he had buried himself under and saw Chuck retracting into his hiding place. Chuck! The big guy on *their* team, courtesy of Jeremy. *'He led them right to us,'* Martin thought fleetingly. Chuck had a hideous smirk on his face. He was laughing. They were all laughing. The low roar of their impervious glee seared his eardrums.

"Got that, boys? We fixin' to play us a good ole game of paintball today," someone shouted into the thick air. It was Jeremy's voice.

"Yeah, your blood will do nicely in place of paint. Those balls don't quite splatter the way blood does, you know? It's just not the same. So we go'n make sure we do this right. Why, we wouldn't want to bring you all the way out here to play a half-assed game. We want to make sure your first game of paintball is the real thing. Your first and your last, that is." He heard Jeremy chuckle and walk away. The crunching of the leaves under his feet became distant, and it sounded like he was walking back towards the common ground. Jeremy might have left, but the others hadn't moved. They were lying in wait, ready to pounce. Waiting...

8

He could hear the laughter emanating from the bushes. He could hear the distant gait of Jeremy's smooth, calm step. He could hear his heart thumping wildly in his chest; he could hear all of these things. He could also hear underneath all the peripheral noise, he could hear Shaun panting heavily, trying desperately to get a handle on himself and the situation. He could hear Craig shaking against the dead leaves. He could hear Gary's soft cries of confusion. Martin heard it all. He covered his ears and sank his head. A deep, guttural yell rose from his diaphragm, shaking his body in anger and dread.

9

It seemed like hours before he moved. He could see Martin's shoulders heaving massively as he sobbed loudly."

God, he wanted to get up and run. He wanted to run for his life. Instead, all he could do was stare at Martin's back as hot tears streamed down his face.

"Shaun? Shaun??" He heard his name whispered in the cool of the unfolding day, and it woke him from the trance he'd slipped into.

"Shaun," Gary pled.

"Yeah, man, yeah. I'm here, man."

Gary inched close to the ground, trying not to make a sound. He crawled over to Martin first and put his arm around him. Martin hadn't moved. His mouth was still open, shaped in the grimace left from his painful shout. Tears had dried on his cheeks, and he dry-heaved sporadically and rapidly. Gary made his way through the fallen leaves to Shaun and said,

"D-D-Did that sh-sh-shit really ha-p-p-p-pen, man? Did you see that sh-sh-shit-t?"

Shaun looked at him vapidly and nodded. Gary was stammering badly. In the seventeen years that they had known each other, Shaun hadn't heard Gary stammer or stutter or trip once. Not once. He grabbed Gary by the shoulders as he shook and said,

"I saw it, man. Good God, I saw Robert go down."

"Where is everybody? Where are they, man? Kevin? Craig? Where-"

"Kevin's dead, G. Kevin's gone, man," Craig said from behind them. Martin looked up slowly from the ball he had rolled his body into. His eyes searched Craig's face, laden with mud and leaves and blood. There was blood on his jacket; it glistened in the dull light that the trees let through.

"Are you hit, C.? You alright, man?" Gary asked him in a

shaky, high-pitched tenor, far from his usual baritone rumble.

Craig looked down at his jacket and said,

"No, it's not my blood. I'm not hit. I was next to Kevin when he went down. I guess I wasn't as far out on the perimeter as I was supposed to be. The shot was so loud, I thought I would never stop hearing the echo. They came from somewhere behind us. They were hiding in the bushes, but there's no way they could have gotten to that position so quickly. It was like he got shot seconds after the game started. It wasn't even a minute after the second whistle blew before they gunned him down."

They looked at each other in silence. Craig touched the blood on his jacket and began to sob.

10

"Where are they now?" the old man asked Jeremy. He looked pleased but on guard. He paced the room, his toeless foot thumping on the floor hard in unison with his wooden cane with each step. A glaze of sweat was forming on his forehead. He laughed heartily before Jeremy could answer and shook his fist towards the window in defiance.

"Who says we don't own this land, huh?" he shouted, "Them niggers think they runnin' us - they think they runnin' everything! They think they such hot shit. We showin' them different, ain't we, boys? We finally putting them in they fuckin' places, yup. This is where they belong. In the jungle, running scared like animals and hiding like cowards and then dying at the hand of a righteous man. A

White man. It's how it always should have been, and would have, if it hadn't been for those bleeding heart bastards and uppity niggers like King and Evers. Fuckin' coons. Too weak to be a buck, so they got book smart. But that book smart shit don't work out here in our place, do it, boys? These fuckin' coon bastards go'n suffer today. And pretty soon our mission will take out all of 'em. All of 'em!"

He raised his hands in the air in triumph, and Jeremy's hands raised to meet them. "There are four left, Dad. We shot two of those fuckers down already. One of 'em spurted his blood all over the leaves out there. Big fuckin' mess."

"Don't worry about it, boy. Nigger blood is better than rain."

Jeremy smiled and patted his dad on the back. He turned to the door and walked into the hallway. He stuck his head out and said,

"Eddie, you ready for part two?"

"Jerry, I don't think we even have to do it. They're easy pickins out there. They ain't got shit for bullets and we got them outnumbered."

"I know, but it'll be that much sweeter to see them fall for our trick. Trust me on this one. You'll see."

11

The four of them sat together in a huddle. The wind was whipping up, and the air was getting cold. How long had they been out there? An hour, maybe two? In that short time, their lives had changed forever.

In the bushes to their front right, they could hear bugs

chirping and buzzing loudly over Robert's body. The hot, pungent smell of fresh blood saturated the air and made it hard to breathe. It was their friends' blood. Robert's and Kevin's. Craig spoke first.

"Look, we don't have anything but paintballs in here. No bullets. We are sitting ducks if we don't run for it. There's no other way." He looked into the clear plastic cover and saw fluorescent pink and yellow paintballs in the hopper. He shook his head. "We've got to go for it."

"What, and give them free target practice?" Shaun exclaimed. His face was covered with sweat and tears. His lips quivered as he spoke.

"We can't just run out there and book it to the cars, hoping to hell none of us gets our asses blown off! Who knows where they are now, just waiting for us to make a fool move like that so they can cut us down."

"He's right," Martin said. He had been silent since Robert's death, unable to speak, unable to think. "We can't just *run* out of here. We need a plan."

They put their heads together to come up with a way out. Splitting up was the only option. They dumped their worthless guns and facemasks and moved within the bushes as quietly as possible, veering off gradually in different directions. The plan was to get to the cars and wait for each other. The first ones to the car were supposed to hide on the floor until all four of them got in. They were going to put the cars in neutral and let them roll down the incline they were parked on. When the cars rolled far enough away from the woods, they would start the engines, and Jeremy and his friends would have to run to catch them. They could escape if they stuck to the plan. They could get out.

12

They moved with very little sound and quickly found themselves alone. Shaun crouched and crawled through prickly tangleweed, wincing from the pain, but not uttering a sound. Then he heard something. He kept going; afraid to stop now...and then he heard it again. A low, jumbled sound was coming from the bushes off to his right. It sounded like moaning. His mind flooded with thoughts of Kevin or Robert lying in the cold mud, colored red by their blood. He thought of one of them gasping for air and mouthing his or one of the other guys's names, begging for help. He whispered,

"Kevin? Kevin man, that you?"

It had to be Kevin if it was anyone at all. He saw Robert get shot with his own eyes. He saw the blood and the distant look in his eyes before he was engulfed by the bushes. He knew Robert couldn't be alive.

No answer. Maybe the wind was playing tricks on him. Maybe he wanted it to be one of his friends so badly that he made himself believe they were calling to him. Maybe... A voice beckoned weakly from the bushes. He moved closer, no longer cognizant of the noise he was making, and asked,

"Kevin? You're alive?"

He pulled back a branch and uncovered Eddie, one of Jeremy's friends. He was bleeding from a shot to his left shoulder. His gun was lying on the ground close to his right foot, and his shirt was ripped to shreds. He was propped unsteadily on the menacing tree stump, his back painfully hunched.

Shaun recoiled quickly and started to run. He could

almost feel the beam of the gun on his back, targeting his heart through his clothes. He was terrified. Eddie wheezed,

"No! Please help me."

Shaun stopped running and turned his head towards Eddie cautiously. Eddie was injured, the pain on his face was unmistakable. He was reaching for Shaun earnestly, wanting - needing help.

Shaun stood in place and said, "You didn't see me, man. Keep it that way." He turned to leave, but Eddie whispered,

"SHH! Be quiet. They're all around here. They're waiting for you - for us."

Shaun looked around him and saw nothing but the twisted branches of trees and evergreen shrubs. He listened intently and heard nothing but the birds vacating the area in search of warmer weather. Getting away. Like he wanted to. He walked towards Eddie and said,

"What do you mean, *us?* You're one of *them.* Why would they be looking for you?" He nudged Eddie's gun away from him and brought it to his side. Eddie let him do it.

"See, man? I'm safe. I'm not with what the other guys are doing." He sucked in air heavily and with marked difficulty. There was blood all over him. It saturated his shirt. He was sweating profusely and shaking slightly. Shaun didn't hold the gun on him, but he kept it close to his side.

"I'm not with them, I swear it. I don't know what's going on. I've known Jeremy for years - ever since we were kids...I don't know what's happening." He breathed in thickly again and coughed. He trembled violently and turned red.

Shaun watched him convulse. He wanted to believe him, but he had to be sure. He said,

"That's bullshit. How could you not know what's going

on? You're one of them! You're on their team! You planned this with them from the start!"

"No, no. I swear, I didn't have any idea this was going to happen. I came out here from Boston to see Jeremy on Friday. He told me he was going to be playing paintball with a couple of friends and a colleague from work. A friendly game, that's all. I never knew there was going to be anything like this. Dear God, if I had known... do you honestly think I would be in this situation if I knew?"

He shifted his weight and gestured towards his wound. Shaun sighed and said,

"Why'd they do that to you, man? Why'd they shoot you and how did you stop them from killing you?"

"Jeremy -" He stifled a sob. "Jeremy shot me. After he shot the first one - your friend - I asked him what the hell was going on. I thought we were just going to play paintball. I had no idea anything like this was going to happen. I told him I wouldn't be involved in this and that I was going to find you guys and help you get out. I told him that what he was doing wasn't right. That it just wasn't right. He -he shot me with absolutely no remorse. He left me to die. He said that he wanted me to suffer, and that he hoped that one of you guys found me and beat me to death. I crawled down here from up the hill. I was trying to get help, but I - I'm so tired. God, man, we've been friends for so long I can't believe - I can't believe what he's doing."

Eddie turned his head away from Shaun and sniffled. He pulled his arm up to his eyes and buried his head in it. Shaun watched him as he went through his pain. He had just lost two of his closest friends, so he understood what Eddie was going through. Eddie's body began to shake. Shaun put his hand on Eddie's shoulder to comfort him. He propped the gun against a tree and covered his own eyes as he let his emotions out. Eddie continued to cry as he quickly put his hand, clad with open handcuffs that were hidden in the bushes, on Shaun's right wrist. Shaun looked up in surprise. The realization that he had been fooled came over him. Before he could process this betrayal - before he could react at all — the hand that held the tears he shed for his lost friends was locked viciously in the cold iron cuff. Shaun couldn't believe what was happening. Eddie's cries of pain and anguish turned into hearty laughter. He stood and exclaimed,

"Whoa, Jerry! You were right! That trick sure as hell did work!" He leaned down and whispered into Shaun's ear.

"Your nigger friend's blood was still warm when I took some and smeared it on my shirt."

Shaun yelled out loud in fear and anger. Eddie continued to laugh as Jeremy came from behind a nearby bush. He smiled at Eddie, pleased with his work, and said,

"Take 'im back to the shed, Eddie. We'll set up the rest of it. Oh, and gag 'im so he cain't shout."

Eddie nodded and giggled as he led dumbfounded Shaun to the shed. Jeremy shouted at the top of his lungs.

" Boys, we got one of yo' nigger friends now. If you want his tired ass, you'll come get 'im at the shed. If all of you ain't there in, oh, say, 15 minutes, we'll kill 'im and skin 'im. Ain't that what happened to that stupid nigger Nat Turner?" He chuckled and said, "You niggers are just as dumb and gullible as they say you are. This shit is easy as taking candy from a baby." He strolled towards the shed, shooting blanks out of Eddie's gun into the air.

13

Martin stopped in his tracks and looked around as Jeremy beckoned for them to come to the shed. They caught someone. Who? How? He sat on the ground and looked at his hands. He didn't know what to do. He knew he had to find the others, if they were still in the woods...if they were still alive.

**

Craig turned around quickly at the end of Jeremy's diatribe. The woods seemed to be closing in on him. The trees seemed to be laughing at him. He suddenly felt very small. The claustrophobia that he had once overcome came back viciously and overtook him. He fell to the ground wide-eyed and unable to breathe sufficiently. He was paralyzed by fear.

**

Gary ran down the hill and out of the consuming wilderness, ignoring Jeremy's call to the shed. He could see the cars up ahead. He was so close, he could almost touch them. He kept running, not once looking back, not even when Jeremy reiterated that he had captured one of his friends, not even when he heard the gunfire. With tears in his eyes, he ran to the Jetta. He fumbled with the keys in his pocket, having trouble grabbing them and pulling them out because his hands were shaking so badly.

There were footsteps behind him. They were rapidly approaching. He could hear the heavy breathing and the wheezing, shaky voice uttering what sounded like his name. Elated, he turned around, thinking that one of his friends had made it out. With a smile he extended his arms, only to see that it was Brad, one of Jeremy's boys. He was holding a double-barrel rifle at his chest. Brad was so close, Gary could feel the edge of the barrel grazing the button on the pocket of his shirt. Gary's smile dissipated, and he said nervously,

"C'mon, man. Let me go. You don't have to kill me, OK? You don't have to do this, man."

Brad looked at him gravely, not moving a muscle in his face. With a placid, strong voice he said,

"Yes, I do."

He pulled the trigger.

14

Martin clawed through the bushes to find his way back to their fort. With no other safe (as if any place was really *safe*) common ground, he hoped that the others would think to meet there after hearing the announcement.

Martin got to the clearing and fell clumsily to the ground, his body wracked with exhaustion and fear. Frantically, he tried to think of who could have been caught. Shaun? Gary? Craig? He didn't know. He tried to be quiet and wait for the others, but his mind was throwing all different kinds of scenarios at him. Could Jeremy have been bluffing, and this was a setup? Did Jeremy really have one of them and, if he did, was he still alive? Martin didn't know. He couldn't believe any of this was happening. It seemed like a dream. One that he couldn't wake himself from. It was a horrible nightmare.

Craig came around the corner huffing and puffing. He looked at Martin and said,

"Where are the others?"

"I don't know. What took you so long to get back?"

"I was out of it, man. The trees, they looked like they were closing in on me. I guess I slipped back into one of those fits I used to have when I was a kid. You know, the ones where I can't move at all, no matter what I do. I snapped out of it a couple of minutes after the gunfire. When I was running back here, I thought I heard more gunfire, but it was off in the distance. Did you hear it?"

Martin nodded solemnly. He heard the shot but hadn't processed it until Craig brought it up. *'My God, did one of us get shot?'* he thought.

"Who do you suppose they have? Gary or Shaun," Craig continued.

"I don't know, but we only have seven minutes or so to get to that shed they were talking about. I hope whoever's left — Shaun or Gary — will go right to the shed. We can't afford to waste anymore time waiting for them."

Martin got up and started to walk into the bushes toward the shed - or in that general direction. Reluctantly, Craig followed behind him, looking back every now and then to see if either Shaun or Gary showed up at their fort. Both Martin and Craig had lost their sense of direction with all the running in circles, and they couldn't recall where the shed was.

They made their way to Jeremy's fort and beyond, still not seeing any sign of the shed. Frustrated and scared with only three minutes left, Martin turned his head up to the sky and shouted,

"Where are you, Jeremy? What the hell do you want from us?"

He threw his arms out to his sides in rage. A sarcastic chuckle came from behind them. Slowly, Jeremy emerged from the woods. It looked almost like he was arriving from another dimension, the way he seemed to glide out and away from the bushes and trees, floating towards them with unnatural grace. He was unarmed and stripped of the bulky garments they had all worn to keep warm during the game. He was sweating bullets, as though he had been running through the woods, tracking their steps. He was smiling demonically, pleased with the cat-and-mouse game he had set up.

Hatred welled in Martin's throat, suffocating his rational thoughts. He lunged at Jeremy, throwing all of his weight at him. Jeremy leaned to the side and tripped Martin. He fell flat on his face. Martin turned over onto his back and looked up at him. Jeremy was *smiling*. Craig went over to Martin and helped him to his feet.

"You 'bout done now? I can stand here and fight you 'till the cows come home, but your friend is going to run out of time. Tick, tock. Tick, tock. The seconds keep a' tickin' away." He turned towards the bushes and started to walk away.

The southern drawl Jeremy was displaying was new to Martin. He had never heard it before that day. He didn't think he would ever forget it. Craig nudged him along, and they followed Jeremy into the woods.

Jeremy had a streak of blood down the back of his grimy T-shirt. It was thick and wide with bits and pieces of flesh on it. Craig gagged as they walked, unable to fathom whose blood that might be. He stumbled and tripped over his feet, falling to the ground. He was feeling the same feeling that plagued him before. The trees were starting to close in on him. They mocked him with intangible laughter and pointed their accusatory fingers at him while he writhed on the floor, gasping for air, precious air.

Martin went to him and raised him to a sitting position. Jeremy was drifting out of sight.

"C'mon, C. Get up, man. We've got to go and save our boy. Please Craig. I don't even see Jeremy anymore. We've got to catch up to him."

Craig tried desperately to catch his breath, but he couldn't. He tried to wave Martin on, but his limbs were heavy. His face turned ashy gray from the lack of oxygen, and he started to fade. Faintly now, he could hear Martin begging him not to die. Telling him to hold on. He could see out of the corner of his eye something - someone lying on the ground next to him, hidden away from sight under the bushes. It was Gary. His eyes were upturned, and his face had a tormented grimace forever etched on it. Without fighting he allowed himself to slip into unconsciousness. He couldn't take any more of what was happening.

15

Martin watched his friend drift off helplessly. He couldn't stay with him; it was already too late. Jeremy had completed disappeared into the brush, and Martin only had one minute left to help his friend. He got up slowly, saying a silent goodbye, and ran in the direction Jeremy was headed, casting a solemn look back at his friend Craig, who lay partially under the bushes.

Martin caught up to Jeremy quickly and said, "How far are we from it, man?"

"Is that nigger friend of yours dead?" Jeremy asked maliciously with his back still turned.

"Yes. He is."

"Bonus. That way I don't have to waste a round on him."

"Is that your plan? To kill us all?" Martin's voice had taken on a shrill quality. It was the sound of panic and disarmament.

Jeremy stopped walking and stood with his back to Martin. He pondered the question for a moment. Suddenly, he lifted his head to the sky and let out a monstrous laugh that shook Martin to his core. He shook his head and turned to look at Martin. With pity in his voice, he said,

"Don't you realize that you are already dead?"

He smiled and turned his back to continue deeper into the woods. He pushed the bushes away, clearing Martin's view of the shed, and of Shaun.

16

Shaun's arms and legs were bound by rope to a wooden cross that was wedged into the ground. He was completely naked. His nipples had been cut off and stuffed up his nostrils, protruding them grotesquely. The jagged lacerations in his skin were bleeding profusely. Sweat covered his body, and he had soiled himself. His head was lowered onto his chest. He had been beaten savagely, and his skin was discolored in several places. Martin was certain that his friend was dead.

Martin saw an old man in the doorway of the shed. His eyes were gleaming. He had a look of contentment and anticipation on his face. Next to him stood Jack, the controller of the firm he and Jeremy worked for. His face was red and sweaty - it held a look of mocking satisfaction. Martin could have killed them. All of them.

Before Martin's eyes, Wally and Kurt poured gasoline on Shaun's limp body. Wally lit a match and threw it on Shaun's stomach. It stuck there until the flame ignited.

"Looks like we's fixin' ta have a right ole' Bar-B-Q, ain't we, nigger," Steve said jovially. Martin was flabbergasted. Everything that he was seeing, everything he had seen, was a blur to him now as he stood incoherently before his friend's burning body.

A bone-chilling scream escaped Shaun's lips, and he lifted his head slowly. He shook on the makeshift cross, trying to tip it over and escape perishing in the flames. Quickly though, he was silent.

Martin snapped back to reality and attacked Kurt, pushing him into the flames with Shaun. Kurt lunged away from Shaun's burning body quickly, but he couldn't escape the flames. They clung to his face and shirt, devouring the skin underneath. He screamed deliriously in pain and threw himself on the ground. He groped for something that would extinguish the flames to no avail. Wally threw a blanket over him and tried to beat the flames out, but it was too late.

"You muthafuckin' bitch," Steve said and grabbed Martin's arms. He threw Martin to the ground and put all his weight on him. Martin shut his eyes. All the fight had drained out of him. He heard all too clearly the cocking of the gun. He felt the cool barrel on his temple and welcomed it.

17

The gunshot woke Craig from his unconscious state. He peered through the dead leaves and roots to see if he could detect any signs of movement. He had to get out of there; he knew that now. He didn't think anyone was left from his crew. The gunshot had to be for Martin; he was sure of it. Gary was dead, Kevin was dead, Robert was dead, Shaun had to be dead. He was the only one left.

He got up and moved slowly at first, cautiously. He could hear them talking loudly and cursing about something. They sounded angry - maybe Martin and Shaun took care of one of them before they were killed. God, he hoped they had gotten at least one of them.

Craig made his way down the hill in virtual silence, blending in with the darkening day and slipping out into oblivion. He made it to the truck and reached for Martin's keys in his pocket. They were warm against his leg. He pulled them out slowly and clenched them tightly in his hand for a moment, unable to stop the memories from flooding back. Unable to say goodbye.

Quietly, he got into the truck, taking pains not to slam the door. He checked the back seats to make sure that no one was in there with him. He ducked under the windows as he slid the car into neutral. As the car rolled backwards down the incline and out of the hardened mud onto the dirt road that led to the main drag. He prayed that there was nothing behind him that he could hit and draw attention to himself. He just wanted to get out.

He felt pebbles crunching under the tires, and the ride became less smooth. He was out of the mud and on some semblance of a road. He turned the ignition, shifted the truck into first gear, and took off. He kicked up rocks with the back tires as he sped down the dirt road, shifting the gears roughly and abruptly.

Craig made his way through the dense brush on either side of the road, positive that one of Jeremy's friends was waiting there for him, gun in hand, aimed and prepared... but they weren't. He made an uncontested right onto the paved road. He saw the faded paintball sign in the rear-view mirror getting smaller and smaller. Tears rolled silently down his cheeks.

Passing him quickly on his left was a red sports utility truck filled with five guys...Black guys. They made a sharp left turn into the paintball area.

\/\\|/\\|/

THE INN BY THE CEMETERY

1

"What do you think it is?" Sharon asked, her eyes squinting at the indiscernible snake-like thing covered in the red Virginia clay that passed for dirt in that part of town. Its sections coiled beneath the caked soil, stilled seemingly from the sheer weight of the reddish-brown clumps that buried it.

"I don't know," Mitch said, his voice airy, almost a whisper. The thing looked like it could be a piece of jewelry, yet it was different than anything he had ever seen. His wife was a fan of bracelets and necklaces, rings and earrings. Almost anything gold caught her eye, and if it contained a diamond, she was enamored with it. He couldn't care less about jewelry, at least for himself. He wore his wedding band and his wedding band alone. That was enough jewelry for him. Still, he indulged his wife as best he could, buying her a piece every now and then because she liked it. And if it made her happy, he was happy. The problem was that now had become then, and the gifts were becoming few and far between. Sharon never complained. She just window-shopped silently, adding things to her mental wish list.

But that thing, the piece lying beneath the clumps of dirt and grass, was suddenly more stunning to him than anything he had ever laid eyes on before. He realized that he was as enthralled with it as Sharon seemed to be. Maybe more. The grit that covered it couldn't conceal its beauty. It was a bracelet of garnets and gold. Its construction was early, maybe early 1800s antique. The detail was meticulous; someone took care in crafting the perfect setting for the pure stones, making sure that each of them sat nicely in the gold and would hug the delicate wrist of the woman who wore it. The garnets were bezel-cut and arranged in the shape of roses. They sat in a base of vermeil, each rose connected to the next by a sliver of gold. He could see the bracelet as though it were clean, its stones gleaming under the light of a chandelier. It was exquisite.

Mitch's mind filled with the aura of the bracelet, setting the scene of a grand ballroom with men dressed in tails and women dressed in their finest gowns, their bodies accentuated with corsets and bustles covered with striped cut velvet. He heard laughter and the sound of music in the background. Sharon reached down to touch the undecipherable thing on the ground. Mitch saw her just as she was about to pick it up. The daydream of times past dissolved as he watched her lean closer to the dirt-covered bracelet.

"Don't touch it!" he said a little louder than he meant to. "It could be anything."

"Like what?" Sharon asked as she knelt down, leaning closer to the coiled thing on the ground. "It looks like a bracelet," she said, her voice rising in the excitement of the find. She got even closer to it, getting down on all fours.

"Mitch, you gotta see this. It's beautiful! It's a bracelet with some sort of red stone..."

Sharon kept talking, but her voice sounded farther and farther away. Mitch's mind drifted back in time to a place where he was dressed to the nines and a regal-looking woman hung on his arm. They entered a room, a large expanse in a private home with hardwood floors and ornate molding framing a high ceiling. A crystal chandelier hung from the center of the ceiling, the colors from the light dancing on the wall.

The room was full of people. A band was perched on the steps that led to the sunken ballroom, attired in the obligatory tails and white gloves. Negro servants stood in the shadows waiting to pick up discarded plates or to refill empty glasses. As he looked on, a manservant named Sammy—

how do I know his name?

—smiled and nodded at him. A chill came over Mitch, and suddenly he could hear Sharon's voice talking at him again.

"... Don't you think? I mean, whoever dropped it is long gone. This thing looks like it was buried in the ground."

Sharon reached her arm out to pick the bracelet up, but Mitch grabbed her arm.

"What?" Sharon said, her voice sounding as exasperated as her face looked. "What's the big deal? It's just an old bracelet. Nobody even cares about it."

"How can you be so sure?" Mitch said, his mind still clouded in a haze of roses and wine.

"Mitch, what are you talking about? Whoever left it is long gone. Look around you. Nobody even comes here anymore. It's just some old, forgotten cemetery."

Her words brought him back to reality and away from

the fantasy world his mind had concocted starring him as the dashing escort at a century-old party. He blinked twice to clear his eyes and ground himself. His gaze tumbled over the tombstones, some crumbling, some sunken. The cemetery was falling apart and indeed looked as if it hadn't been visited by friend or family in decades. An old church sat at the far end of the land behind the tombstones. Reedy vines crawled up the building's façade. The constant beating of wind and rain had weathered the structure, soiling the exterior and eroding the carvings. The place looked as though it had been standing for centuries. It was sturdy, like the relics in Europe.

The church was the reason they were standing there among the graves. A spontaneous weekend trip brought them to town and to an inn that had opened in 1909. Mitch never wanted to stay at an inn or a bed and breakfast, for that matter, but it was on Sharon's list of "life experiences". Mitch thought he was ingenious when he picked the place. She wants to experience staying at an Inn? She's got it. She wants to experience staying at a Bed and Breakfast? She's got that too. The Inn they were staying in was originally opened as a Bed and Breakfast until converting to an Inn five years prior. There you have it. Two "life experiences" down. God knew how many more "life experiences" she had left to put him through.

Sharon noticed the cemetery as soon as they got to the Inn. The large slabs of stone, the mini George Washington monuments, the statues of Mary looking mournfully down at the ground — presumably put there to console the sorrowful loved ones left behind. All those things were lost on him. Cemeteries were places for the dead and no place for the living to hang out in, or even look at too long. He had felt that way for years. Ever since he was a kid. When Mitch was seven, his grandfather died of a heart attack. He had been close to his grandpa, so he wanted to be a big boy and say goodbye like everyone else did. He sat through the open casket funeral with the body displayed full couch, managing not to get up and run out of the room even though he wanted to—every time he looked at his grandfather lying in the casket it was like the world zoned out, faded into a static kaleidoscope, and all Mitch could see was his profile. He didn't hear the minister talking about the reward in Heaven, didn't hear the sniffles and sobs coming from the people in the congregation. He only saw the side of his grandfather's face. Even from his seat, Mitch could tell that his grandfather's face was as hard as stone. It didn't look natural. The lines he'd had around his mouth when he smiled were pulled taut, the hair in his beard seemed to lack the luster that it always possessed. In fact, it seemed that he could see each individual hair reaching out from the bulb embedded in his chin. His eyes were probably the most troubling of all. The top eyelid was pulled to his bottom lid tightly and, between the gray lashes, Mitch could see a glint of the glue picked up by the light. It looked like his grandfather's eyes were tearing, but Mitch knew better. But still, it looked that way.

The rest of the congregation mourned the loss of Carlton J. Richards, lamenting over him with exclamations of 'Lord Jesus' and 'Help, Lord' peppering the ceremony, but Mitch was far away from them. The body of his grandfather intrigued him, possessed him somehow. Mitch was stuck there, staring at his lifeless face, powerless to turn away until the force field was broken. He did this for a while, staring without blinking for what seemed like minutes before finally looking away, released by the same unseen force that held him in place a second before. And then his grandfather turned toward him.

Mitch could hear the sound of his grandfather's bones creaking, snapping, breaking as he turned his neck to face him. His eyes and mouth were still closed, but Mitch could see his lips working to open into a smile. Finally, his grandfather snapped the thread that had been sewn into his lips to keep his mouth closed. It hung from his lips like disturbed cobwebs. He arched his eyebrows and rolled his dry eyes in their sockets until the glue that held his eyes closed cracked. Mitch watched as his grandfather blinked once, twice, three times as though he was trying to clear his eyes. Mitch's eyes cascaded to his grandfather's chest and saw that it was still. At that same moment, his grandfather unfolded his hands with some effort and put his right one on the edge of the bronze-colored casket in which he lay. He sat up, a deep, guttural groan emitting from his chest as he did it and scanned the room with his withering eyes.

Then he swung his right leg over the side of the casket.

Mitch screamed out loud then and stood up from his chair. His mother put her hand on his back, rubbing in smooth gentle circles the way she always did when he was upset. She was saying something, but Mitch didn't hear her. His eyes were focused on the body of his grandfather again, lying in the casket as though nothing had happened. His hands were folded across his lap in the unnatural way undertakers like to position the dead. His eyes and mouth were closed. Mitch sat down more out of shock than embarrassment. No one really paid attention to his outburst other than his parents. Everyone else was wrapped up in their own grief display. His was just a number in the act, and a relatively weak performance at that. Mitch never looked at his grandfather's face again after the funeral. Not even in pictures. He was afraid of what he might see playing at the edges.

When Sharon mentioned the tombstones, her enthusiasm was met with a dull mumble. She didn't let it bother her. She studied history in college and had worked on her family's genealogy, tracing her mother's line all the way back to the mid-1500s. She discovered while she was looking for family tree connections at a cemetery bearing her family's surname that the old dates on the tombstones fascinated her. She tended to view the world as if things just happened recently, certainly no more than one hundred years prior to her birth. It wasn't something she was conscious of initially, not until that day in the cemetery. She was amazed one day, when surfing the Internet, to find out that homosexuals had been persecuted in Germany in the early 1900s, and ancient civilizations had been advanced enough to create what are now the ruins at Chichen Itza—whole cities with homes, religious buildings, centers, and even out of the home eating areas. In her mind, people who lived that long ago didn't—couldn't—have had the same struggles, stresses, or issues that people experienced in the present. Not that she found earlier generations lacking in capability; it wasn't that at all. She just didn't see far beyond her scope of things. What was prevalent in her generation just couldn't have been an issue way back when. Her mind couldn't grasp it.

The same went for lifespan. Everything she had been taught in history books showed that people who lived in the 1700 and 1800s didn't live long. They typically died in their mid to late forties. The first time she saw the tombstone of a person who was born in 1789 and died in 1882, she was floored! She stood in front of the woman's chipped tombstone and read the dates over and over. She started to imagine the life she might have had. Sharon's mind replayed the historical events that took place while the woman, Mrs. Eleanor Patterson according to the stone that marked her grave, was alive and wondered how they might have affected her. Before she knew it, she had spent half an hour standing in front of the grave of a woman to whom she was not related.

From then on, she was hooked. Whenever her genealogical research took her to a cemetery, she went early in the morning, excited about the dates she might find, the lives she might envision. One leg of her family line brought her to the property of a renowned slave owner in North Carolina. She drove three hours from Washington, DC, to Henderson, North Carolina, wondering all the while what she might find there aside from her relative's tombstone. After about an hour of rubbing the tombstones she needed and taking pictures of the plots themselves, she happened upon a wooded, unkempt area with large rocks scattered about. Some of them had sunk into the ground. Almost all of them were covered with childlike handwriting that was all but worn away.

A slave cemetery.

2

Running in tandem with her genealogy research, Sharon looked into the slaves and the owners of North Carolina, trying to pinpoint whose graves she had found interred on the land. After long hours and a year of solid research, she found the name of one of the slaves buried there. Priscilla. Sharon spent days dreaming up a life for Priscilla. She wondered if she worked in the fields or in the main house, if she was dark or light-skinned, if she longed for freedom or carried her burden in silence. Priscilla consumed Sharon's thoughts, so much so that she decided to write a book about her. Sharon's novel <u>Of Life and Death</u> was due out the following February. To say that traipsing along in a cemetery was right up her alley was an understatement.

They checked into the quaint inn, its décor done in antique rustic, an interesting combination that worked somehow. They took the stairs up two flights to their spacious room, opened the tall wooden door, and breathed in the soothing smell of cedar.

The door opened onto a large sitting room with a window running the length of the back wall. A carved walnut settee with a rose embroidered cushion sat beneath the window with reading lamps on either side atop end tables. A pair of striped high-backed chairs sat opposite the settee. The floors were a deep brown hardwood, and a portion of the floor in the sitting area was covered with a sectional rug. The bedroom was to the right of the sitting room, at the end of a long, narrow hallway. A writing table stood flush against the wall closest to the doorway. A cherry wood armoire stood opposite the writing table, its scalloped carvings and pierced apron prominent in the light of the setting sun that trickled in from the window opposite it. A queen-sized, Spanish iron-framed bed took up most of the room with its tall mattress and assortment of throw pillows. The room was incredible.

"Isn't this great?" Sharon asked, unable to conceal her excitement as she flopped onto the bed. Mitch looked at her, at the smile on her face as she scanned the room. God, he loved her, her love of life, her exuberance. She was like a breath of fresh air. And her excitement was contagious.

"Yeah, it is kind of neat, that is, if you like bed and breakfasts."

Sharon shoved him playfully and said, "I already know your game. You think because this used to be a bed and breakfast you're killing two birds with one stone. Not a chance."

"Why not?" He pointed to the bed and said, "Here's the bed." He picked up the room service menu and found the breakfast section. "And here's breakfast. Get it? Bed," he pointed again, "and breakfast. And the name of this former bed-and-breakfast is now The Dandelion Inn, so that covers the Inn part. I don't see the problem."

Sharon smiled even wider as he tried to combine the two experiences. He talked a good game, but she knew he enjoyed their little escapades as much as she did. She picked up one of the throw pillows from the bed and threw it at him.

"Sorry Charlie. No dice on this one."

Mitch walked toward the bed and leaned over her. He could smell her perfume. It was just the slightest bit sour, mixed with her sweat. It drove him crazy. He licked his lips as he let his eyes linger on her lips, full and moist, ready to kiss his.

"I can think of other ways to get the pillows off this bed."

"Really," Sharon said, her voice catching in her throat. "Why don't you show me?"

3

Mitch woke up to find himself alone in bed. The sound of the shower was muffled—the bathroom was all the way at the other end of the hallway near the front door. The sheet was bunched between his legs the way it was when he fell asleep. He had a tendency to stay still while he slept. Sharon, on the other hand, was restless. She would kick the covers off and knock her pillow to the floor. But he stayed in the same position he drifted off in. He smiled at the memory of Sharon that flooded his mind. In the beginning of their relationship, she thought he was pulling her leg about his sedentary sleep. She would watch him fall asleep, staying up as long as she could keep her eyes open to try to catch him moving. She even went as far as to set up a camera to tape him while he slept. She played the video the next morning when they ate breakfast, sure she was going to prove him wrong and expose his little trick. She watched all six hours of the tape that day to try to catch him, but she couldn't. There was no movement other than the rise and fall of his chest when he breathed. She called him a freak when the tape was over. *Who knows? Maybe she's right*, he thought.

Mitch got out of bed and walked toward the window. He was contemplating joining Sharon in the shower to start round two. In their four years of marriage, they had never done it in the shower of a bed-and-breakfast/inn. They could add it to their list of "life experiences".

Mitch was about to turn down the hallway and jump in with Sharon when the small window in their bedroom caught his eye. He turned and walked over to it without realizing what he was doing. It was dark, with a light fog hovering over the street, but that wasn't what had caught his eye. The cemetery they passed when they turned into the Inn's parking lot was right across the street from them. Seeing the tombstones reaching toward the night sky, their shapes accented by the dull yellow light from the streetlamp on the corner, made him feel uneasy. His skin felt clammy, chilly, as though a draft had just swept through the room. He touched his forehead and felt a film of sweat at his hairline. There were so many of them, markers of the dead. His mind lurched toward images of decaying skin and tattered rags; horror movie depictions flooded his head. He could feel them; the weight of their death pressing down on him. He could see their hands clawing furiously at the dirt, could hear their bones cracking as they strained to pull themselves up, could hear their moans of discontent. His chin trembled as he watched them moving, milling, haunting their burial place.

Then he saw her.

She stood in the center of the fray of ghostly figures, her countenance clearer than the others. Almost solid. She wore a dress in a deep shade of wine, almost indecipherable against the backdrop of the night, with a plunging neckline that showed her ample cleavage. The folds of the dress were full, and the length was long, but he knew somehow that the legs beneath were slender and smooth. Her hair was pulled up with ringlets of dark brown cresting the top. Her delicate neck was adorned with a beautiful necklace of intricate design, garnet and gold, the stones shaped like roses, the gold so thin as to not be seen.

He could see her, her face, her body, clearly, as though she were standing in front of him in the room rather than through the glass, two stories down, and across the street. Her features intensified the longer he looked. Fear lingered around the edge of his consciousness.

She smiled at him as he watched her, at home among the dead, yet appearing different from them. Her lips were painted with the sultriest of reds, pouting ever so lightly around the edges. She ran a hand from the hollow of her throat between her breasts, down to where her belly button would be, all the while looking at him, calling to him with her eyes. Mitch could feel himself rising as he watched her. The thought frightened him at first, but arousal wiped the fear away. He didn't hear the water in the shower stop running, nor did he hear the sound of Sharon's feet on the hardwood floor as she approached him from behind.

Sharon slapped Mitch on the right buttock; his bare cheeks too hard to resist. The smack jolted Mitch's attention from the woman in the cemetery to Sharon. He turned to her, his eyes wide and wild-looking. The smile on Sharon's face quickly dissipated when she saw him.

"My God, Mitch, you look like you just saw a ghost! Are you ok?"

Mitch released the air he had been holding in his lungs and realized that he hadn't taken a breath since walking over to the window. He looked back at the window and saw that the other ghosts had disappeared, leaving her alone in the cemetery. Her mouth was open slightly as she darted her tongue over her lips, moistening them. Mitch felt Sharon move from behind him to his side. He thought about blocking her view of the cemetery but moved too late.

"Oh yeah, the cemetery is right across the street. I saw that when I got up."

Mitch looked at Sharon incredulously. Couldn't she see the woman in the cemetery? She was staring right at them!

The woman looked at Sharon with eyes that blazed red. She cast one last glance at Mitch before turning her back and walking deeper into the cemetery, among the graves. She seemed to fade as she walked, disappearing altogether within seconds. She was gone.

Mitch looked at Sharon again and realized that she

hadn't seen anything at all. The woman had only shown herself to him for some reason. He shivered unconsciously.

"You ok?" Sharon asked, walking away from the window. "It doesn't bother you, does it? The cemetery."

Mitch swallowed and tried to find his voice. "I'm ok."

"I mean, I know you don't like them and all, but they're harmless," she said as she squeezed lotion from the bottle and applied it to her leg.

"It's not like ghosts come out of their graves at night to prey upon the people who stay in this inn or anything," she continued, "although that might make an awesome movie." She laughed. Mitch could barely force out a chuckle.

"There's no boogeyman or anything like that. It's just a place where people put their loved ones after they die. A resting place. Nothing more, nothing less," she finished.

"I know," he offered weakly. He knew what he had just seen, and it haunted his thoughts. As his thoughts wandered back to his grandfather's funeral, he couldn't help but wonder if maybe the dead never truly rested.

"I'm going to take a shower," Mitch said over his shoulder as he started towards the bathroom.

"Good. Maybe when you're done, we can have another go in the sack." She smiled playfully at him, her naked body lying on top of the beautiful bed, positioned seductively. All he could do was smile at her. He didn't much feel like having sex anymore—

at least, not with her

his mind echoed. At least, not with her.

4

After he got out of the shower, he and Sharon made love

again. He could tell that she wasn't as satisfied with their second romp as she had been with their first, but he was able to cry fatigue and leave it at that. That was one of the joys of marriage. Occasional sexual inadequacy was accepted and ignored; passed off as nothing. There was no more trying to prove yourself, trying to make it perfect every time. Marriage gives you the do-over option.

After sex, they ordered dinner in. Sharon fell asleep about an hour after dinner and was still sleeping when he opened his eyes to the dark room. He stared at her while she drifted to sleep, watched her eyelids flutter when she started to dream, watched the rise and fall of her chest as she breathed. He would never let anything happen to her; he knew that then with a clarity so sharp, it was painful. Nothing would ever touch her if he had anything to do with it. Not man nor animal. Or spirit.

Mitch woke up again at two o'clock in the morning. The quaint little room they'd rented at the Inn had lost its appeal in the dark shadows of early morning. Mitch heard the floorboards creaking in the room above them. Apparently, some lucky couple was making good on their weekend escape instead of sleeping the night away. *Good for them*, he said under his breath. At least somebody was having a good time. The neighbors in the room next to theirs weren't faring quite as well. Mitch could hear the woman sobbing as her husband/boyfriend/date spoke demeaning, cutting words in the most angry, stentorian voice he could muster. Mitch felt sorry for the woman. He was happy that Sharon was sleeping soundly next time him, unaware of the argument in the next room. She would have felt terrible for the woman and would have dreaded going into the hallway or lobby the next day on the off chance that they would meet. She'd be afraid the woman would show her embarrassment on her face, would know somehow that Sharon was in the next room and had overheard everything. Sharon would then feel uncomfortable knowing that she had heard it, and so the cycle would go until they left the Inn for home. Mitch was glad that Sharon slept like a log, for once.

The darkness in the room seemed impenetrable, palpable almost, like it could swallow him whole if he stepped into it. His eyes struggled to see, to get used to the darkness and make out the furniture, their clothes strewn on the floor, anything. After what seemed like forever, his eyes cleared. He could see the chair and lamp that sat by the window, the dresser, the edge of the rug. He started to feel a little better when his vision opened up, unconsciously unfurrowing his brow and relaxing back into the pillows. He hadn't realized that he had sat up in bed to scan the room, looking for something, anything decipherable in the dark. It wasn't the same, the dark at the Inn. It was different than the dark in his bedroom back in Herndon, VA, even with a wooded lot surrounding the house. The dark didn't seem as heavy, as tangible, at home. It didn't feel as if it were teeming with unseen creatures that were lurking there, just beyond his view, waiting for him to step off the bed and into their world. Mitch chuckled to himself, but his laughter sounded on edge. *This is silly*, he told himself. *You're a grown man! You can't be afraid of the dark!* But the dark at The Dandelion Inn was different. It was alive.

Mitch could see the floor plant standing in the corner of the room, engulfed in the shadows of the night, its shape resembling that of a voluptuous woman. The vision beyond the window came back to him then, the woman who had been standing in the cemetery earlier that night. The memory of her didn't frighten or startle him; instead, it warmed him, made him stir. She was beautiful, a sight to behold. He remembered her eyes, her lips so full and inviting. His mind allowed him to forget the ghosts that danced around her and the fact that he saw her appear out of thin air. Instead, it reminded him that it was her that he wanted to see that evening. And he couldn't deny it.

He indulged in the fantasy, shutting his eyes to the odd room, and stepping into a white-walled space with a bed and soft music playing that existed only in his mind. She came to him there, dressed not in the wine dress she wore in the cemetery, but in a short black silk gown with spaghetti straps and lace. Her hair was down, loosened from the bun, and resting lightly on her shoulders. The soft curls caressed her cheeks and forehead. Her eyes, the same rich brown as her hair, looked seductively at him from behind thick eyelashes. Her lips were colored with the same luscious red.

She stood in the doorway of the room looking at him as he lay on the bed. He was erect from the very sight of her, wanting to go to her, but knowing that he couldn't. This was her game, and it would be played by the rules that she set forth, and none other. He looked at himself and could almost see the throbbing of his rushing blood coursing through it.

She took leisurely steps toward him, rolling her hips as her weight shifted, drawing out her approach. She enjoyed his look of desire, his impatience; she could smell his lust on his skin.

She crawled onto the bed on all fours, giving him a view of her cleavage as she did. Mitch reached for her, and his hand met with the softest skin he had ever touched. He kissed her hungrily, pressing his mouth to hers, and darting his tongue inside her mouth. He couldn't control himself. He needed to touch her. She returned the kiss with passion, slowing him down, controlling their rhythm. Her mouth satisfied him more than any other kiss had ever done. Her hands upon his chest gave him chills. He moaned under his breath.

The woman pushed him away abruptly, catching him off guard and leaving him longing for her touch. She knelt in front of him with her back slightly arched, pointing her pert nipples toward the ceiling. She ran her hand over her left breast slowly, caressing herself, seeming to savor the curve, the feel of the satin that covered her skin.

Her hand moved slowly, sensually, up to her neck. It was smooth with only a small blemish on otherwise clear skin: a perfectly round mole. Her brown hair fell in wisps around her neck, blowing in the faint breeze that encircled them where they lay, a breeze he couldn't feel. He thought his sensibilities might be swirling in the breeze also, funneling like a tornado, whipping like the winds of a hurricane.

A gleaming red suddenly took his attention away from the travels of her hand, making him focus on the base of her neck. A choker of garnets and gold rested just above her collarbones. The necklace was intricately designed with little clusters of garnets bound together in rows of three. The rich color of the gemstones seemed to pulse in time with the beating of his heart. He watched as the flash of light intensified as his own heart rate sped up with desire.

Her wrist bore the complement to the necklace; strung garnets clustered and bound to a sister set with the thinnest of gold. It too pulsed with the beat of his heart, hypnotizing him. A smile formed on her lips as he was drawn into her spell. She pulled gently at the spaghetti straps on her shoulders, letting them drop just above the elbow. The gown slid effortlessly from her body. Her nakedness was mind-blowing; her body seemingly the most perfect one he had ever laid eyes on. Her breasts were round and firm, her stomach was flat, her hips were wide, and her legs were slender. She had the most perfect hourglass shape he had ever seen. He couldn't help but put his hands on her waist, her shoulders, her thighs, anywhere and everywhere he could. He needed to feel her curves beneath his palm.

She crawled over him, leaving his skin feeling tingly from the touch of her skin on his. She pressed her lips to his, and his mouth felt refreshed and cool. He put his hands on her hips, just above her buttocks, and moved her body back and forth. She didn't resist. Another moan escaped his lips and died in her kiss.

He sat up, turned, and pulled her body beneath his. Her hair splayed across the pillow, framing her face angelically. She smiled sensually, closing her eyes in anticipation of his lips on hers, pulling him to her through some unseen force. He was happy to oblige and kissed her once more, running his fingers through her soft hair.

He felt his hips gyrating slower and slower as he prepared to enter her. He wanted to feel her, all of her, and do it slowly. The shifting of the mattress is not what turned his attention, but the cough that neither he nor the woman beneath him had emitted. Mitch looked to his left and saw Sharon's blanket-covered body shifting in her sleep. Her hand rubbed her nose, making a squishing sound—a telltale sign that she would wake up in the morning with the beginnings of a cold. He remembered that she had complained of a draft earlier in the day. It was then that he felt the air he knew to be swirling around him. Around them. A cool wind with such a crisp edge as to raise goosebumps on the flesh.

He felt them rising on his skin as he watched his wife rub her nose in her sleep. Sharon sniffled once and then drifted back into her dream state, never having opened her eyes.

Mitch turned back to the woman beneath him only to find that she was gone. His eyes took in the inn as it had been before the dream: a dark, shadowy room. The white-walled room of his daydream disappeared the moment he heard Sharon's cough. He looked for the woman anyway, peering the darkness, trying to make out her shape. He caught a glimpse of his reflection in the mirror. He was on his knees with his right arm extended and leaning into the bed. He held his penis in his left hand, still erect. The space beneath him was empty except for rumpled sheets and a pillow.

Mitch eased himself back into his place on the bed, being careful not to bounce the mattress and wake Sharon. He controlled his breathing and the beating of his heart. He felt himself relax; the pulsating desire he had in his loins dissipated with the elapsed time. He looked over at Sharon's back; her nightshirt was bunched up and wrinkled, her hair a tangle around her head.

The wind was gone.

The stillness of the room was like static electricity to him. His eyes darted around the room more in fear than confusion. But fear of what? Of a woman who seduced him in his dreams?

His eyes glanced at the window at the other end of the room. It was smaller than the one in the living room, but he could still see the tops of some of the taller monuments in the cemetery. He could almost hear a voice calling him, moaning seductively in the night. He turned his eyes away with great effort. A chill covered his skin. He shivered as he settled deeper into the bed, pulling the covers over his shoulders.

Mitch stared at the end of the bed, looking at the hump his feet made under the covers for a long time. He was afraid to look anywhere else in the room and afraid to close his eyes. After a while of cowering in bed like a child after a nightmare, a chiding chuckle rose in his throat and spilled out into the darkened room. He admonished himself again for being such a 'fraidy cat. His voice was the only sound; the neighbors upstairs had apparently turned in for the night, and the one's next door had quieted down. The sound of his voice bounced off the floors and walls. There was something wrong with it, though. On the surface, it was jovial, like the laughter behind a good joke. But at its core, it was edgy and ragged.

"What's so funny?" Sharon asked in a sleepy voice, her eyes still closed as she turned toward him and nuzzled his arm.

"Nothing baby. I'm sorry I woke you," he said, bringing his voice down to a whisper. He ran his hand through her hair and said, "Go back to sleep."

Sharon nodded and drifted back to a full sleep with ease. Mitch kept touching her hair, feeling the texture, and remembering the woman in his dream. *That's what it had to be*, he told himself, *the best damned wet dream I ever had*. He laughed again, but this time it held no humor.

5

The next morning, Mitch woke up to find Sharon already out of bed. He called to her, feeling uncomfortable in the bed by himself, feeling uncomfortable in the room itself.

"I'm out here," she replied from the living room. He knew why she was there. She was looking over at the cemetery. She would want to go there before they left, to walk among the graves and concoct fantasy lives for the people in them. He'd have to oblige her, after all, her imagination thrived on things like that. Half an hour in the cemetery could be fodder for her next book. He only hoped that she wouldn't make him stay any longer than that.

Mitch got out of bed and met her in the living room. Her face was awash in sunlight as she looked out at the cemetery across the street. He couldn't resist kissing her on the cheek; she looked so gorgeous in the morning. He forced the memory of his dream girl, lips parted, waiting for him to kiss her, out of his mind.

"Whatcha lookin' at?" he asked, trying to affect a light tone. He kissed her cheek and the side of her neck playfully.

"See that cemetery over there? Right across the street?"

How could I miss it, he replied in his mind, but managed to keep his response to Sharon even. "Yeah."

"There's a neat old church back there behind the graves. I've been thinking of a plot for a short story the whole time I've been standing here. You know, nineteenth-century demon possession, haunted land, pre-*Night of the Living Dead* kind of story. I thought it might be neat to check it out. Go in, walk around. It doesn't look like anyone has been there in years, at least from here. It might be kind of spooky. It could give me some great ideas. You up for a good scare?" She poked playfully at his ribs, giggling at the idea of Mitch in a creepy church surrounded by a cemetery.

"What? You don't think I can handle it?" he said with his best try at machismo. He puffed out his chest and said, "I can take anything. It's you I'm worried about."

"Great. Let's get dressed. I really want to check the place out. I feel an evening of writing coming on!"

Sharon bound into the bathroom and within seconds, Mitch heard the shower running. *Damn*, he thought to himself, and looked over at the cemetery grounds, its tombstones gleaming in the morning light.

6

They found the church door closed, welded shut. All the windows were boarded up, and the stained-glass murals were broken. The stone was cold, uninviting. Mitch found himself wanting to leave the place because of the church as much as for the cemetery. But Sharon ooed and ahed, genuinely enjoying the "life experience".

"Look at the doors, Mitch. They must be hundreds of years old!" She stood looking up at them, with their high arches and ornate hinges. They looked creepy to him.

"I wonder what the stained glass might have looked like." Sharon strolled the length of the church talking about what could be inside, what services might have been held there. By the time she came back to the front where Mitch had remained, she was wondering about the congregation.

"What did they look like? What might they have worn to church? What was happening in their lives when they belonged to this church? You know?"

She was rattling on by then, and Mitch knew better than to answer her rhetorical questions. She really wasn't looking for his input. She was just talking. It was interesting to see, really, because this was her way of creating an outline. She was organizing her thoughts for her next piece, rounding it out without pen or paper.

Sharon started walking away from the church and toward the graves. It was just like Mitch thought it would be.

He knew they would end up looking at tombstones after a while. It was inevitable.

"Who is buried here? Members of the congregation? People in town? Fallen soldiers? Maybe the town rogue, whose family owned a plot here? Maybe the harlot who no one ever looked in the eye?" Her voice sounded farther and farther away as she walked up and down the rows of tombs, stepping over broken monuments, walking around sunken plots. Mitch stood where he was, at the end of the footpath to the church, ready to leave. There was a chill in the air, and he found that goose bumps had risen on his skin. The bumps made him think of the previous night, and he glanced quickly at the inn, seeing what he thought might be the window in their bedroom.

Standing there in front of an old church in the middle of a graveyard, Mitch wished he had never picked that particular Inn, the Inn by the cemetery, with an unobstructed view. He wanted to leave, to forget the place existed.

"Mitch," Sharon called from up ahead. "Mitch, come here!"

His heart sank when he heard her voice. His mind called up the images of the night before, the ghosts that crawled out of their graves to walk the cemetery, the woman who stood looking at them in their room. The woman who visited him in the wee hours of the morning. He remembered the look on the woman's face when Sharon peered out of the window in her direction, standing next to Mitch. The look of anger was indescribable. Her eyes had burned with a fury unknown to humans. But there was something more, wasn't there? Something else behind the anger, the jealousy that shot from the woman's eyes. It was a look of possession.

Mitch ran through the cemetery toward the sound of

Sharon's voice, imagining the ghosts on either side of him cheering, laughing as he went. He finally found her around the side of the church, bent over a tombstone. There were no ghosts, no swirling beings surrounding her as she read the writing on the tombstone. There was no woman standing over her with vengeance etched on her transparent face.

Mitch felt the pressure lift from his shoulders, and he looked at Sharon's body, bent at the waist, engrossed in the etching on the tombstone in front of her. It was all in his head. His mind had been playing tricks on him since they started the trip. He decided then that he wouldn't visit another cemetery with Sharon, except for funerals. His imagination ran wild when he did, and for him, that wasn't a good thing. He decided he had to tell her that visiting the cemetery could be checked off his "life experiences" list. Been there, done that. As he walked toward her, he realized that his argument might actually work.

Sharon turned to him with excited eyes and said,

"Look at this, Mitch! Elizabeth Mabry, born March 31, 1717, died March 17, 1817." She paused for a moment, waiting for a reaction. Mitch stood silent, a feeling of dread coming over him again. His eyes caught sight of something that his mind couldn't believe, couldn't fathom.

Sharon didn't notice. "This woman almost lived for 100 years! Only two weeks more and she would have been 100 years old! That is incredible! I mean, we're talking about the 1700s! The life expectancy couldn't have been more than forty-five!"

Mitch tried to smile while Sharon looked at him, but he wasn't sure if he had pulled it off. Sharon didn't care; she was off in a world of what-ifs and how dids, imagining a life for the woman whose grave they stood over, romanticizing a death that happened two hundred fifty years before they were born.

The story she designed made Elizabeth Mabry the wife of a rich landowner, an affluent developer of his time. She socialized with all the right people and went to all the important balls and parties. She wore beautiful gowns and stunning jewelry, setting the pace for the socialites of the era to follow. Mitch's head reeled as Sharon described her life, a life that he saw with vivid clarity, as if he were recalling a memory of his own.

"Look at this, Mitch," Sharon said, cutting her description of the life of Elizabeth Mabry short. "What do you think it is?"

The bracelet that the woman in his dream wore on her wrist lay at the base of Elizabeth Mabry's tombstone; its pure garnet stones pulsing bright red through the Virginia clay, in time with the beat of his heart.

BLIP

"WHAT THE HELL?"

Laurie couldn't stop herself from saying it, even though she'd been trying not to curse as much since life had changed and the kids were now at home during the day. But it was hard, harder than it should have been – harder than she would ever admit out loud that it was. Oh, who was she fooling? Everybody in the house knew she was having a hard time keeping her language PC. Some days she gave up trying before lunch. But this time she had been in the middle of a report, and yes, she had saved it, but not in the past five minutes, and she had been on a roll typing, cutting and pasting, damnit, she was almost finished. So, yeah, she cursed out loud. 'Hell' wasn't as bad as what she almost let slip.

"Nooooooo!" was the call from downstairs from a voice that sounded a lot deeper now than it had when the pandemic started, a voice that was attached to a kid who was also taller than he had been before the world went to hell in a handbasket – a kid who was taller than her now. That wasn't saying much with her being all of 5'4", but still. Seven months ago, she was looking him in the eye, and now she most definitely was not.

The other one didn't say anything- probably didn't even notice anything because she was on her phone. It seemed like overnight the phone had fused with her hand like an appendage, and even though she couldn't make calls on it yet, she could do everything else: learn makeup tips from people who painted theirs faces to look like cheetahs and then somehow made it all come together into something beautiful, listen to songs that teetered on the edge of questionable, the lyrics clipped just before parents' ears would perk up and pay attention, fawn over some boy band from another country and learn words that nobody else in the house understood. Thank you, COVID-19, for the premature teenaging.

The hum of the house kicked back on not even three seconds after it turned off, adding insult to injury because she knew it was too damned late to salvage anything. Because Laurie wasn't using her laptop, not right then – she was signed into a meeting on her laptop, but the report she was writing was being created on her desktop. Why? Because she was a dinosaur, that's why, and she was kicking herself for it now. The laptop hummed along during the power surge, only offering a slight hesitation when the power cut off - just enough to miss a word or two from the fast-talking New Yorker who didn't know the answer to the question he had been asked, but was trying to talk himself toward some kind of solution, anyway. The laptop, thanks to its nifty battery pack, stayed on while her desktop summarily cut off, no fade to black for good ole' Betsy, no, just now you see it, now you don't. When the power came back Betsy waited for Laurie to boot her back up, the old bitch, and Laurie obliged, knowing what she would find – the saved copy of the work she had completed before her coffee break, all formatted and spellchecked to boot – ooh, she could be so anal about things sometimes – but the work she had completed in the past few minutes were gone with the wind.

Laurie remembered when she and Rob had talked about homeschooling – remembered how she was dead set against it. And there were so many reasons to be against it, she thought as she listened to the CPU booting up again, hoping the power stayed on long enough for her to email the document she had been working on to her work email so she could finish it on her laptop, but she had her doubts. There were at least seven other households filled to the gills on her street alone thanks to the pandemic, and that was nothing compared to what it would look like when everybody had to give up the ghost and stay home. They had to vie for connectivity and power all day, things that were usually in abundant supply. When the world was normal, there were only maybe 35 people working from home in their 400-house community. But now, with just about half of her community (which ended up being more representative of her county and even her state than she ever expected) having their kids go to school online at home, there were more people than she could identify by face toiling around in their houses. Sometimes she looked out of her window and saw people taking walks, which was normal under any circumstance, but these were people she had never laid eyes on before. People she had never seen in the supermarket, in the restaurants on what they called restaurant row, the cleaners. Not even in Target, and it seemed like everybody she knew or knew of in her little town ended up at Target at least once a week. When the pandemic hit and people started to work from home or lost their jobs or whatever happened to them, there were people milling about that she hadn't even known existed.

The Punjabi family.

The couple speaking what she thought might have been Dutch and walking at a fast clip, no doubt racking up steps on their Fitbits.

The Nigerian grandmother who taught her how to say, 'I love you' in Yoruba after Laurie heard her yelling, "Mo ni ife re!" to her children as they drove away (that was before things got too bad. Laurie couldn't help but wonder if she has seen them since, thinks she should maybe check in on the woman to see if she needed anything).

Laurie was also getting used to people's habits - like the guy who drank coffee on his front porch in his bathrobe, come rain or shine, and the kid who rode his bike down the middle of the road, always popping a wheelie where it curved.

Every. Single. Day.

She had even stopped being startled by the family - all five of them... mom, dad, daughter, and two sons, each under the age of 10 – who took their daily walk at 2:30 in the morning. Laurie had to believe there was a reason for it being so late–maybe the dad worked the night shift or the mom worked overnight in one of the big box stores. It couldn't be that they were a bunch of vampires, looking for somebody's blood to suck... right...?

They weren't... hunting for meat yet, were they?

It couldn't have come down to that already... right?

No, of course not. The bigger question, and she had to remind herself about this often enough, was why she was up to see them on their daily jaunt in the first place.

Dogs barked.

Cars passed by.

All seemingly on cue.

Sometimes she felt like whipping her head around fast to try and catch the camera crew recording her life like she was the new Truman in The Truman Show: Pandemic Style. That would be strange but so was staying six feet away from everybody and wearing masks every time you stepped outside and looking up recipes to make hand sanitizer because you can't find any in the stores.

Blip.

Careful Miss, your slip is showing.

Booting up slowly but booting up.

The boy still yelling downstairs, so close to dropping a curse of his own, she thinks she almost hears it, wonders distantly if she'll say anything about it if it does fall out of his mouth or if she'll let it slide this time. Rob was lucky he missed all this stuff, if you could call that lucky. He's usually stuck at work, the firefighters sleeping on the job, bunking together like they were in dorms. When she was feeling sentimental, she thought he might actually miss them, miss their little family and all the noise that came with it. But then she imagined booze, and ashtrays overflowing with butts, tables filled with takeout wrappers, video games, and porn playing on the big screen, and she realized how silly she had been.

Kid stomping up the stairs.

The man-child coming.

Taller, taller. Laurie had time to think that if her daughter, curiously silent but almost looking her right in the eye at age 11, kept growing at the rate she currently was, she'd be taller than Laurie in a year or so before her son started in.

"It's so messed up!" he said, pacing in front of her, the sound he made against the floor too loud for what she envisioned coming from his six-year-old feet. "I was in the middle of a match!"

"It was a power surg-"

"I know, Mom, but I was in the middle of a match! We couldn't get on all day – somebody always had something else to do – and now, when we *finally* get in, this happens."

Oh God, what will we do if we miss the match?!

It's been ALL DAY LONG, even though all day amounts to maybe two hours now, at noon.

My life will be over if I can't get into this match, you don't understand, for real, no cap, honest, on the real, yo, you just don't get it, man.

A smile crept onto Laurie's lips as she considered the back and forth that could happen if she responded the wrong way. It was comical, really, how worked up he could get over matches and arsenals and power packs and whatever else went on in the world of the game he and his friends connected in. And she supposed that was ok. Because stuck in the house like they were, that world was his world, at least for right now. And in that world, he could run around outside and jump off stuff and break down doors and dance over people when he did it. Just like in her daughter's world, she could learn dances and post them and get likes and thank people for them and then do it all over again.

"Jes-" Laurie started, but the man-child cut her off again with more of his ranting.

"- Dave is like never on-"

Probably because his parents find other things for him to do. They are better parents than me, I guess.

She shook her head and knew he didn't understand why, and that was ok.

It was still quiet upstairs.

But not where Laurie was. No, not at all.

"-planned since yesterday," Bobby continued, "and now it's all messed u-."

"Jessie?" Laurie yelled up the stairs like she did so often, letting her voice carry rather than climbing them.

Her son kept talking, undeterred. He was flapping his arms, nearly flinging himself around the foyer.

Laurie thought the stench that every parent stuck in the house with kids aged 10 and over knew all too well might knock her out.

No answer.

"Jess- Bobby, hang on a second, ok?"

Teeth sucking.

Sighing.

Laurie almost laughed.

"Jessie, honey?"

... what? Are you ok? That's what Laurie wanted to ask for some reason, but why? What could be wrong? Jessie was upstairs looking at her phone like usual, and from where she was, likely on her bed propped up on that furry armchair pillow thing on her bed that's on its last legs, nothing had even happened. If she had her earbuds in, Jessie hadn't even heard Laurie call her name.

Technology... gotta love it.

"Mom!" Bobby groaned, and for some reason Laurie was accosted with the memory of his father catching his toe on something as they waded into the water in, where was that, Aruba? Barbados? She couldn't remember. She had been waiting for him to get in the water – he took his sweet time putting on sunscreen and putting his hat and sunglasses somewhere safe so they wouldn't fly away, get up and walk away – whatever it was he was afraid of. Everything he was doing was so slow and methodical. Laurie thought she was going to jump out of her skin. She wanted to get in the water, to feel the sand between her toes, to taste the saltiness of it on her lips. And when they finally waded in, when the vacation finally started to feel real, Laurie heard Rob scream. Laurie didn't remember if it sounded exactly the same as Bobby did as he called out to her in complete and total frustration, but it might as well have. And from underwater on some sunny day in her past, how was she to know that she would hear that sound again, somewhere down the line from the kid who calls the screamer 'dad', his namesake, as melodramatic as he was. She dove underwater that day, acting like she didn't hear him, buying herself maybe a minute more of bliss. She wished there were something to duck under right then.

"What if I can't get back in-."

"Go check," Laurie said, before looking at her computer to make sure they had connectivity and that he could actually log in. She just wanted him out of there, wanted to stop the onslaught of his yelling and the funk of not washing in days because nobody was going anywhere, wanted to silence the grating pitch voice was taking on. And that was ok. She wasn't up for the Mother of the Year award anyway, not this year, "but go check on Jessie first," she heard herself saying.

Laurie hadn't looked away from the door, hadn't realized she was planning to send her first up to see about her second, but she had done it and now it was out there. Bobby sighed again and mumbled something under his breath, but started toward the stairs anyway, calling Jessie's name once more, hoping she'd save him the trip. When he settled down enough to notice, Bobby could see that there was something about the way Laurie was staring up at the stairs from behind her desk, hardly moving a muscle, that didn't allow any room for questions.

If Laurie had ever had the chance to tell the story, she would have said that Bobby, her sweet boy who looked like her uncle more and more every day with his hair, growing long in the quarantine, but not unpleasantly so, only made it up one stair before it happened. She would have said that they were both taken aback because he had been in the basement and she had been on the main floor and Jessie most certainly had not been on either of those. She would have had to have been to be where she was right then, but she hadn't been – they were sure of it. But there she was, outside, looking at them through the window, the vanes open just enough to let in some light but closed enough to keep out some of the heat that sometimes came on fall afternoons out, those days when Laurie found herself dressing and redressing, trying to keep up with weather that was inherently schizophrenic during that time of year. There she was, outside the house with no way of getting there, unless she had climbed out of her window and jumped down. But she couldn't have done that either, and just walked away from it. And besides, the alarm hadn't gone off when Jessie opened the window... *if* she had opened the window... which she couldn't have... Laurie was sure about that too.

Jessie was smiling.

A dog was walking.

The power walking elderly couple were pumping their arms, their neon orange weights glowing as they went about their normal routine.

Bobby was on the stairs.

Jessie was smiling but there were too many teeth. Too many in her preteen mouth, too many for an adult's.

Something wet was dripping, pooling somewhere on a carpet; the wet, plopping sound was deafening.

There was a whine, something faint, almost not there. Like a sound caught in the back of someone's throat when the thing they were most afraid of looked like it might really be coming for them, like a dog who knew it was trapped and begs for mercy because it ought to but knows it won't get it.

Like the sound of the electricity going out everywhere, for the last time.

Lips working, undulating, pulling back to reveal bloody gums, puckering out in a grotesque kiss and through it all, she was smiling, her lips splitting, gore spilling out, all mucus and pus tinged with red.

The lights flickered.

The power turned off again.

One

Two

Three

"Ghaawwwwdddd, *what?*" Jessie yelled and flung open her bedroom door to find her brother standing in a pool of urine and her mother's mouth open so wide it was as if her jaw had distended, unhinged, broken. They were staring at the window, staring so intensely that they hadn't heard her... until they weren't.

Laurie and Bobby whipped their heads toward Jessie so fast, Bobby lost his balance and fell against the wall. She would have laughed were it not for the looks on their faces. Surprise – like really, she scared the hell out of Bobby and deep down, she was happy about that. At least he actually *saw* her for once – ever since they had been locked away in their house, Bobby had only noticed her if she was standing in front of the TV. But it was more than just surprise. There was also confusion on their faces, like they didn't understand what they were looking at. And something else, though it took her brain a few cycles to get to it – fear.

They were afraid.

Black lines in front of her eyes, encasing Bobby and her mother too. Black lines like borders on a picture, like bars on a jail cell. Shimmering, waving, moving, like hot meeting cold on an abandoned blacktop

Four

and it was getting darker around them, darker around her mother, blurring her face behind it, creeping into her open mouth. Jessie called to them, but they didn't hear her. She reached out, but her hand met the black bars instead, and they felt solid even as her hand dove into them as if they were water, sank in there and tingled in the unseen space.

The cellphone in her other hand was warm, so warm, too warm.

Her hand was in the bars, disappeared at the wrist and prickling like it had fallen asleep... like a thousand needles were bouncing off of it – not penetrating, but bouncing, bouncing, bouncing like her hand was a trampoline and the needles were who had been stuck inside the house for too long.

Jessie yanked her hand back, and it wouldn't come, it wouldn't come, and she screamed for her momma and her brother, and they didn't hea-

Blip.

ISSUE

1

"Wʜᴀᴛ ᴛʜᴇ ʜᴇʟʟ?"

"That's a big boy right there."

"At least the fucker got off."

"That's always important."

The cops snickered as the coroner's assistant took pictures of 50-year-old Mitchell Pinegrove. Pinegrove had been about 5'11", 230 pounds. He was a teacher at the local high school and lived with his ailing mother. He was found dangling in his bathroom from a noose made from one of his best neckties. He was naked, his body graying center mass, darkening to black in his extremities where the blood had gathered. He was holding his penis in his hand.

"He's a bagger," one of the cops said, flexing his investigational muscles.

"Really? How'd you figure that out?" Charlie Carver asked as he walked toward Pinegrove's body. "Couldn't have been the bag on his head, could it?" Carver and his partner had been the first car dispatched to the Pinegrove home. He had known Mitchell well enough; he taught his daughter's 10th grade science class a couple of years back. Carver had never pegged Cassie's teacher to be the kind to get off on breath play, but then again, he'd never understood why anyone did. Sure, Carver had a dick like every other guy, and he could understand beating off every now and again. He did it himself. But to choke yourself while doing it? Carver was all for getting as much pleasure as he could, but autoerotic asphyxia seemed extreme to him. "To each his own," he muttered under his breath, shaking his head.

Carver was trying to make detective, so he was scrutinizing the case a little more than the other guys were. All they saw was some freak hanging from the showerhead in the bathroom with his dick in his hand. They pitied him, laughed at him for his stupidity, his loneliness. They silently thanked God they could get a date or had a wife to go home to when they felt like getting it on. But Carver saw more than that. Much more.

"The mother says this guy was 50 years old on his last birthday," Jackson, Carver's partner, said. "Isn't that a bit old for this kind of thing? Usually, it's high school kids that do this."

"Not if you're lonely."

Carver stood in front of Pinegrove's blue, distended face and sighed. The plastic bag covering his head, the tie around his neck, the position he was found in: it all leaned toward him killing himself by accident, but Carver didn't buy it. It would be a day or two before the coroner's report would reveal ligature marks around both of Pinegrove's wrists and even longer for the tests to raise doubt whether the plastic bag was on his head before he died or put there as an afterthought, but Carver already knew something wasn't right with the case. He didn't think Pinegrove killed himself, but the lack of sperm on his hand wasn't the only reason. He could feel it inside, gnawing at him like termites on wood.

2

Morris wondered if he'd given too much away already. What he could see clearly was that his first foray into the story was filled with errors. He sighed as he thought about all the fact-checking and theory-proofing that lay ahead. He was nervous starting this, his third book. His first two books, 'A Man Alone' and 'Fallen Angel', had been huge successes. Everybody seemed to want another Mo White mystery. After writing the first book, he sat down to write the second one within three days. But the time between novels two and three was vast—seven months. He hadn't so much as thought about a third novel for five of those months. He was enjoying his newfound celebrity. And why shouldn't he? he thought. It's what he had been working for. He got invited to premieres and low to mid-level Hollywood bashes. After the first Mo White mystery was optioned for a screenplay, he was suddenly part of the 'in' crowd, and he loved every minute of it. One day he was begging the girl next door for a date; the next day he was waking up beside models and aspiring actresses who knew how to play the part. Morris was living the life.

As he stared at the computer screen glowing in the all-encompassing darkness that shrouds 5:00 a.m., Morris started to wonder if he had been partying a little too much.

Carver, his old pal, his trusty wannabe detective, was feeling more like a stranger to him than he had when Morris had first brought him to life. Morris was having trouble sorting out his feelings, his motivation for this next book, and that was bad. If there was anything Morris needed to know going into a new story, it was the why. Without it, the story could never move forward. He couldn't just sit in front of a keyboard and go for it. He had to know where he would end up and why the 'big thing' that was supposed to happen later on in the story would come to pass. Usually, the why came pretty easily. Right after coming up with an ending—putting the cart before the horse, as his mother called it—Morris usually figured out the why. It hung out there like a beam of light from a lighthouse, just waiting for acknowledgment. It didn't take much effort. But that day, as the blank Word screen glowed in the dark, he couldn't see the why. Hell, he couldn't see the who, what, where, when, or how either.

"Shit." Morris cursed under his breath. Usually, when what he refused to call writer's block hit, Morris fancied that Carver cursed too, his New York accent hardening the edge all the more. But either Carver was asleep, or he just didn't give a damn that morning because he didn't say a word.

Morris pushed himself away from the desk, the wheels on the chair sounding incredibly loud as they moved along the plastic carpet guard. He trudged into the bathroom like a man asleep. Writer's block did that to him. Not being able to write was akin to being in a tranquilizer-induced fog, and Morris' body reacted in kind, barely moving the muscles necessary to get him to and fro. He ran the cold water and splashed some of it onto his face. He stared into his eyes as he let the water drip from his sleepy countenance back into the sink, only somewhat aware that the basin was overflowing. He looked like shit, he surmised after studying the bags under his eyes and the pallid tone of his skin. Maybe 5:00 a.m. was too early to get started after all.

The water in the basin rose to meet his hands where they rested on the sides, but he didn't move. There was something in his eyes that had snagged him, that called his attention, all of it. The world around him was beginning to white out, as though a bright light had been turned on, obscuring the shower curtain behind him, his neck, his face. He could only see his eyes, the whites streaked with red from months of fast fun, the brown irises seeming abnormally large and smooth. He only had a second to wonder where the ridges that make up the iris were before he saw Pinegrove hanging from his neck in the reflection. He flinched, but only slightly, as the room behind him changed from opaque nothingness to a crowded bedroom where the body of a middle-aged man hung by the neck. And there was Carver, looking at Morris with an intensity in his eyes that commanded heeding. Finish me, Carver said, his lips barely moving. No one else in the room seemed to have heard him. They continued to mill around the body aimlessly, touching everything and nothing at once. Even the coroner seemed to be idling, walking around the body with his camera retaking shots he had just completed. And then, all of a sudden, the image was gone.

The smile spread across his face before he knew it. It was the one he hated, the one that always frightened him away from the mirror. It was a smile that he was almost positive was not his own, but the resurgence of some 'thing' inside him that only came out during episodes like that, when Morris wasn't in control. Morris turned off the faucet and dropped a towel onto the floor, averting his eyes from the mirror. He was afraid to see that face—his face—again. Sitting down to the keyboard, he got started right away, new ideas flooding in with every keystroke. Carver was back. The fact that the voice Carver used wasn't one that Morris had ever heard before never registered; his rapid-fire ideas were all that were important. Morris and Carver had a case to solve.

3

Carver knew the detective on the case—Jenny had been a friend of his since high school. More than a friend, really, but that was ancient history. At least, for her it was. She still looked good to him. Even though he was married with two kids at home, she still made him stir. He loved to see her when she was intense; the cute way her brow furrowed over her gorgeous brown eyes always made him wonder 'what if'. The tapered business slacks that hugged her curves didn't help either. But that day, Carver had other things on his mind. He couldn't stop thinking about Pinegrove hanging from his neck in his bathroom.

"What did the coroner's report say, Jen?" Carver asked as he sidled up to Jenny's desk and took a seat.

"Why do you care so much, Charlie? Haven't you moved on to bigger and better things?" Jenny was buried behind stacks of paper. Carver tried to figure out which stack was Pinegrove's.

"I knew this guy. He was Cassie's teacher, for chrissakes."

"All the more reason to stay out of this." Jenny could be hard when she needed to be. But Carver knew how to soften her up.

"Something about this thing is sticking with me, is all. I

feel for the poor guy." He could see the ice melting before Jenny said anything. The charm worked every time.

With a sigh, Jenny acquiesced, "All right, Charlie. Take a look for yourself."

Charlie flashed his best appreciative smile, even though it took everything he had not to snatch the folder from her hands. Jenny turned to her computer and started banging away on the keyboard, muttering something about finishing a report under her breath. Carver snatched a glance at her again, checking out her profile as he did often when she wasn't looking. *Damn, she's still a looker*, he thought. *Shit.*

Carver was right. His hunches never lied.

"This is why they put you on it?" Carver asked as he finished the report.

"Bingo. The ligature marks could go all the way back to the guy we're after in New Paltz. The marks on the victim's hands in NP were similar to this DOA. Might have been made with the same kind of material. We're checking fibers now."

Carver nodded absently, his mind focusing on another detail of the report. He wondered if Jenny noticed it.

"Where's the jizz?"

"What?"

"The semen. The report says he ejaculated before death. So where is it? There wasn't any on his hand, and I didn't see any on the floor—."

"You looked?" Jenny tried to hide her amusement as she turned to look at him.

"Yeah, I looked." Carver smiled the way only Jenny could make him, broad and uninhibited. "I'm a cop. I'm supposed to."

"I really think you need to sit for the Detective exam,

Charlie," Jenny said as she turned back to the monitor. "You'd pass it in a heartbeat."

Carver blushed. He couldn't help it.

"So, what about the sperm? What if he shot, and it landed on the wall or on the bathroom rug? What if his mother saw it and cleaned it up, trying to protect her son?"

"Come on, Jen. The man was 50 years old. He'd be lucky if the shit didn't trickle out like water." Jenny wanted so badly to keep a straight face but was failing. "I doubt he shot that far," Carver continued. "But if he did, and it landed on the floor, that would be the last thing his mother would worry about. The bag on his head, his nakedness in general would have been tended to first. The sperm would have been an afterthought, you know? I mean, if you were in her situation, which would you pick?"

Jen nodded in agreement. "So, what are you thinking?"

"Someone took the sperm. For what, I don't know."

"Mrs. Pinegrove didn't say anyone else was in the house."

"Maybe she didn't know."

Jenny turned back to Carver, looking him right in the eye. It made him a little nervous. And a little excited. "It's a rambler, like your mom's place. What, 1500 square feet at the most? She'd hear someone if they were in the house. Hell, even the neighbors would know!"

Every once in a while, Jenny brought up the past, something about Carver that she remembered. It always made him drift into the past, thinking about when they were a couple. Back then she was the only girl that 'got' him. She knew he was more than just a jock. She knew that he was deeper than that, more introspective than the average guy in school. And she liked it. All the other girls he dated wanted him because he was on the football team. But Jenny really cared, really saw him for who he was.

Damn, he missed her.

"Yeah, but she's old, Jen," he said, trying to push the memories away. "And it was 12:30 when we got there. If she turned in early, she might not have known."

Nibbling on a pencil, Jenny pondered that. She added, "Maybe Pinegrove had a date over and was trying to be quiet?"

"Are you saying that maybe he was kinky?" He wondered if Jenny was kinky now.

"If you don't have to get off by yourself but you let yourself be tied up like that, you might be," she replied.

She said might. Yeah, Carver decided, Jenny *was* kinky. He shifted in his seat.

"So, Pinegrove gets a date, brings her to the house, engages in, let's call it, foreplay, and what? She—."

"Or he," Jenny admonished.

"Or he," Carver said reluctantly. He couldn't imagine Pinegrove as gay, but then again, he wouldn't have thought he would find him hanging dead in the bathroom with his dick in his hands either. "Whoever. They get evil all of a sudden and let him die? Or is that person too caught up in pleasuring themselves to realize that old Mitchell was kicking the bucket?"

"Or was it planned? Staged?"

"By who? The lover? Pinegrove? The mother?"

A wry smile spread over Jenny's lips. "The murderer."

Jenny turned back to the monitor and started punching at the keys again. "Do us both a favor and take the test," she called over her shoulder as Carver got up.

"Yeah, yeah," Carver said as he walked away, a new bee in his bonnet.

4

Morris was moving slower than he wanted to on the new novel. That rush of ideas was short-lived. He couldn't seem to get into a groove. Normally he could bang out five to ten pages every two hours, but now he was stuck at one, maybe two, if any. There were days when relaxing by the pool or going to dinner with the new love of his life seemed more exciting than sitting down and writing. He had just met her; the magic hadn't worn off yet. He loved everything about her; the way her hair smelled, the way her lips curved when she laughed—everything. He didn't want to do anything but be with her, lie near her, feed her, sleep with her, snuggle with her—whatever it was, it had to be done with her. Rose Marie. God, she was perfect!

He could rationalize his procrastination too. Who knew when the gravy train would end? Maybe this was the high point. Maybe this was his time. He shouldn't waste it. He should live it up while he still had a chance, while his name still resonated pleasantly on the critics' lips.

Something about the way the new Mo White mystery was going didn't sit well with him either. Things were happening. Lines were being written that he was sure weren't his own. Sure, he told many a fan that he gets into his characters, starts to think the way they would, becomes them to the point that he requires downtime after each book just to find himself again. It worked with the chicks who only read a line or two of text from anyone's book, let alone his. The intellectuals? Well, he didn't imagine they would read his stuff, anyway. But this story was becoming too real, too strange. Like, what was the deal with the sperm? He had made his bad guys collect things before—a finger (the middle one, to be precise) for the serial killer, a tongue for the gangster, a heart for the Bocor—the standard stuff. But sperm? What the hell would the murderer want with sperm? For some reason, even thinking about the storyline freaked Morris out.

Carver and his newest case would be there for Morris when he was ready to jump back in. Right now, Morris decided, he would live a little.

5

Carver and Jackson had just finished lunch when a call came in over the radio.

"We're close. Let's go," Jackson said as he started driving toward the address. They got out of the car and were met by a hysterical man in front of the house.

"She's in there. My-my wife, she's in there. Oh my God, how could this have happened?" The man's face was wet with tears, and his gait was shaky. He started to walk toward the house to show Carver and Jackson where the body was, but Jackson stopped him, urging him to remain outside. It didn't take much. The man sat down on his steps with an audible thump and held his head in his hands.

When they entered the home, they found a woman pinned to the floor. She had bled out long before they had gotten there, before her husband came home and found her. A piano leg had been thrust through her stomach and out her back to penetrate the floorboards beneath her.

"What the fuck? What kind of person could have done this?" Jackson said, his voice tense, edgy.

"A stronger one than you or me," Carver answered in awe.

Carver inspected the piano leg and found that the top was splintered, rough. "Looks like he wrenched this leg free with his bare hands."

"What would make someone do this? I mean, kill her like this?"

"Takes all kinds, my friend."

Carver and Jackson hung around while the team collected evidence and dusted for prints. Carver did a little snooping—just enough to satisfy his curiosity, but not enough to get in anyone's way. The woman had only been married to the guy on the front steps for a year. They were thinking about starting a family, based on all the baby magazines in the bedroom on her side of the bed. Did the piano leg in the stomach have anything to do with that?

Maybe the husband didn't want kids as much as she thought he did. Maybe the husband took it out on her after she told him she was pregnant. *If* she was pregnant, that is. Or maybe she didn't want kids, and the side of the bed Carver had been looking at was the husband's. Carver dismissed the thought. He couldn't imagine the guy out front being the type to buy a bunch of baby magazines and coo over them before drifting off to sleep. He'd been wrong before, but he didn't think he was wrong about that. Anyhow, if he followed that train of thought, the wife would have taken herself out. Carver could think of plenty of ways to off yourself if you really wanted to—he had seen more of them than he liked to remember. Plunging a piano leg into your stomach didn't make the list. No, somebody killed her, more than likely, because she was pregnant. But why?

The husband told Carver that his wife had something to tell him, but that she was waiting until their anniversary that weekend. "I think she's pregnant," the husband said, profound loss coating his words. "My Jenny, I think she was pregnant."

An unwanted thought flitted through Carver's mind, and once it showed itself, Carver couldn't shake the implications it left in its wake.

Two bizarre crime scenes.

Then the name.

Jenny.

Carver shivered involuntarily.

6

Morris shelved the novel for weeks, deciding instead to travel the world. He saw London, Switzerland, and Brussels. He went to the Caribbean and South America to soak up the sun. He never gave Carver, Jenny, or any of his other characters a second thought. Life was good, and he wanted to experience all it had to offer.

When Morris came home from his trip, he languished around the house, avoiding the novel at all costs. He always found something else to do, something else that required his attention immediately. The book sat for months without a single word being added. But inevitably, his insides were getting restless. Morris wasn't surprised, not really. After all, the book was a part of him.

7

Jenny being in trouble—such a stretch of the imagination. Carver knew it, but it was the only thing he would allow himself to think. He didn't want to admit that his desire for her, to feel her soft skin beneath his calloused hands, was bringing on unhealthy thoughts. Admitting that would show weakness, and that was something he would never do. Even when he found himself outside Jenny's house that night, watching her bedroom window as avidly as a peeping tom might, he wouldn't admit it. He called himself protecting her, though she was capable of protecting herself. He was only watching out for a friend.

The office was buzzing the next day. Another dead body was found in a compromising position—a man was found dead on a makeshift sex table equipped with metal ties and harnesses in the basement of the library. Though he was yet unidentified—the skin on his face had been cut away with a razor—the common thought was that it was Lyle Coleman, early fifties, head librarian.

Two men in positions that could be considered reputable with personalities that could be deemed kindly, if not meek, were found in compromising positions at their death. Sexual positions. That their fantasies could drive them beyond the breaking point, reputation be damned, was not a stretch in Carver's mind. Not really. He had a fantasy or two of his own that might raise the eyebrows of those around him. But to the point of death? He wasn't so sure about that.

Who, then? Who would murder these men, men in midlife with no spouses and no prospects? Men with jobs that required patience and compassion, and in so demonstrating, made them quiet and tame. Men whose deaths would shock the community because of the compromising positions they were found in and, of course, their proximity to the children. And speaking of children, why was it that both men's sperm was removed from the scene as soon as they had spilled it? Lyle Coleman's testicles had even been sliced and bled. Could a man do that to himself under the guise of pleasure seeking? Carver doubted it.

A jilted lover perhaps, or an admirer whose advances had been thwarted, maybe? But neither man had been dating. Lyle had never dated, at least his coworkers claimed. And Mitchell had lost interest in the fairer sex since his divorce six years ago. Internet dating? Maybe so, given the times. But for some reason the jilted lover theory didn't resonate for Carver. Call it instinct, but he thought it was something else.

A student, perhaps? Maybe a kid was getting a bad grade in Pinegrove's class, snuck in the house and found Pinegrove in a compromising position. It would be easy to slip the bag over Pinegrove's head while he hung. But then what about the ligature marks? Pinegrove had been tied up before dying and let free to bring himself to orgasm. Carver rationalized that if you buy the theory that the mother heard nothing at all, and Pinegrove had someone with him when he hung himself, then maybe that person snuck out before the mother came downstairs, fleeing so as not to be caught. Why would they run away? Married woman? Married man? Frightened kid?

And what about Coleman? Surely the same student couldn't be having an affair with the librarian. Or could they? Both men were older, but not too old. Both dressed in a distinguished fashion—sport coat and slacks, polished shoes.

Both men had a similar look—short cut hair, graying slightly, same height and weight, give or take a few pounds. It might be feasible. But why kill Coleman? He couldn't affect a grade, so maybe the student idea is out the window. Maybe he threatened to tell the husband or the wife of his lover about their affair and was killed before he could? Could both Pinegrove and Coleman pose a threat to the same person within weeks of each other?

Unlikely.

There was something else.

Carver sat in front of Jenny's house trying to figure out the connection between Pinegrove and Coleman. Aside from the sexual position of their bodies, there was none. Or was there?

8

The doctor visit was no fun. Morris' carefree lifestyle had bought him a nice case of chlamydia. He wished he knew which bitch had given it to him. He kept trying to think back to when it started hurting to urinate. The doctor said that there are, oftentimes, no symptoms of it, that it could have been in his body for years. Yeah, well, he *had* been fucking around for years, and it had finally caught up with him. He couldn't have kids. He didn't know how much he wanted them until they told him he could never have them. He felt as if his life was over.

What was the point of anything anymore? Sure, he wasn't at the point of settling down, not yet. But he always knew he wanted a house, a wife, 2.5 children, and a black Lab for the kids to play with. He wanted a family. And now all of that was gone.

He was depressed. He spent days sitting at home alone. He didn't answer his phone, didn't answer the knock at the door. He told Rose Marie to go and find someone else. He told her about the disease and made sure she got herself checked out. Thank God, she wasn't affected. But after that, he made her leave, made her promise to forget about him. Why should he bring her down? She wanted kids too, and he knew he could never give them to her. So, he let her go to find someone who could.

He didn't accept his agent's phone calls either. Why should he? What was the point in busting his hump to finish a book made up of meaningless words? Even if he made money on it, what was he going to do with it? He had already seen everything he wanted to see, gone everywhere he wanted to go. Without a family to leave the money to, what good was it? Morris turned over in bed when the phone rang, not caring who might be on the other end.

9

Jenny saw Carver pull up in front of her house and came outside. He wondered if she knew he watched her every night, wondered if she liked it. The thought made him excited.

"What are you doing here, Charlie?" Jenny's voice was crisp, aggravated.

"What?"

"In front of my house. What are you doing out here? I saw you here the other night too. Why?"

Carver bristled at her reaction, more than a little annoyed that she was speaking to him that way. Didn't she know he was there to protect her?

"I just stopped by to say hello and you came out. That's all." He cursed himself for sounding like such a wuss.

"Bullshit, Charlie, you've been sitting out here for the past couple of days. And I want to know why."

Jenny was starting to raise her voice. Carver couldn't have that.

"Jenny, settle down."

"Charlie, you better tell me why you're out here or I'll have to call the Captain."

Carver gave Jenny his best smile, and like usual, it disarmed her. "I've been out here because I was concerned for you."

Jenny sighed, but she believed him. "What are you talking about?"

"I didn't want to tell you about this, but I guess I have to now. You caught me."

"That's why I'm a detective. What's all this about?"

He had her. "Just this case the other day. Really, all of them recently. There's something tying these people together, but I just don't know what."

"Yeah, but what does that have to do with me and why you've been out here in front of my house doing a crappy job of hiding? I gotta tell ya, your stakeout practices have got to be better than this if you want to make detective."

Her laughter sealed it. "It's just—her name was Jenny."

"Who?"

"The case midweek. You know, the woman who was found dead with the piano leg stuck in her. That was her name—Jenny. It just—it seems a little strange."

Jenny's chuckle was genuine. "Charlie Carver, you think too much." Charlie smiled and looked down into his lap. It might have been an endearing look to her, but he was just making sure he had settled down enough to get out of the car. "Come inside and let's get something to drink since you're here."

They drank beer and ordered pizza. They talked about old times and people, high school and what happened after. There wasn't sadness in Jenny's voice, just a longing that Carver hadn't noticed before, hadn't allowed himself to hear. That he was a married man was not a topic for discussion, not a topic to ponder. At least not then. Who knew what would happen later? Who cared?

Jenny didn't talk much about men. She didn't seem to have any use for them, no time for the games that men play. Work was her life, and she was happy with that. Or tried to be, at least.

Charlie couldn't have hoped for better. Jenny got herself blitzed enough to accept a pass. Charlie wondered if she hadn't made the pass first, subtly, but there, true enough. She kissed him like she hadn't kissed in a long time. Carver suspected she hadn't. He took her up to the bedroom and made love to her the way he had wanted to for years—hard, fast, unyielding, the way she liked it. It was like heaven. Like rebirth.

10

Morris was working at fever pitch. He poured every waking moment into the book. It was like a light switch went on, casting away the shadows of his lost legacy, obliterating the burning in his loins. Morris didn't think about asking Rose Marie to come over to celebrate his lifted malaise, didn't consider going to a bar and toasting his writing streak with a buddy. All he wanted—all he could think about—was the book. He threw himself into it, adding his blood, sweat, and tears to every word. It satisfied him the way Rose Marie never had. Morris coddled the pages he printed off, laying them next to his bed, touching them like a mother might a child as it drifted to sleep. He was possessed of it, and he knew it.

The scary thing was that he liked it.

11

Jenny turning up pregnant was the least of Carver's worries. Keeping his wife from finding out was the problem. He wanted her to keep the baby, to have his child. But she didn't. To her, being pregnant was like a death sentence. No amount of talking could seem to change her mind, either. Jenny wanted to get rid of the baby—his baby—no matter what.

"How could you want this?" Jenny asked him incredulously. "This baby could ruin your life."

"No, Jenny, don't you see? This is perfect for us. It's the way it should have always been."

"Charlie, you're a married man, for God's sakes! Are you crazy?"

"I love you, Jenny."

Jenny shook her head in disbelief. "You fucking idiot. This is not going to happen."

Carver had heard it all before.

"I'm not having this baby, Charlie."

"Of course you will. It will be beautiful." Charlie

grabbed Jenny's arm, putting more pressure on it than he should have.

"Charlie, you're crazy."

"You *will* have our baby, Jenny."

The look in Charlie's eyes frightened Jenny, filled her with base horror. "Get the hell off me, Charlie."

"It will be wonderful, you'll see."

"Charlie," Jenny almost growled. "Leave me alone. I will do what I want with this baby, and you will have nothing more to say about it, or your wife will find out."

The threat stunned Carver, and he loosened his grip. Jenny snatched her arm away from him and walked off. Watching her go burned Carver up inside.

How dare she threaten him?

She wouldn't do anything to their baby. She couldn't. He'd see to that.

12

Morris' dreams that night were hazy, clouded. It started with him and Rose Marie. He was pounding her with an intensity he had rarely exhibited. It was exhilarating to hear her scream for more, to press him further into her as she gyrated against him. Sex had never been as good as that between them. His orgasm was more disappointing than fulfilling; he wanted more of her.

But then she was gone, and he was in a different place, a different time. He could still feel the tingle of climaxing in his thighs and the balls of his feet. He could still smell her, the tangy sweetness of her sex, caressing his nostrils. A blackness surrounded him that was as heavy as an overcoat, though the air was crisp. He was doing a book signing in a field. His table was surrounded by tall, overgrown grass and weeds. A line of fans snaked through the field as far as the eye could see. He'd be happy to draw a crowd a quarter of that size at a real live event.

Morris was signing copies of the last Mo White mystery. He was cranking them out too, doing his best 'S&S', as he liked to call it (signing and smiling), as quickly as possible. He hadn't looked up to see the people in front of him until a fly rose from someone's hand to buzz in his face. Swatting the fly away, Morris finally laid eyes on the people in line, the ones who would wait in such a secluded place to get him to sign their books. The woman in front of him smiled shyly, her hand fluttering up to her mouth to hide her girlish, toothless grin as it spread across her decaying face. A fingernail dropped from a fingertip filled with pus and discharge. The nail landed on the title page of the new book. It was painted the color of blood. The nail alone was disturbing enough, but the fact that he recognized the woman sent Morris into a panic.

The pleasant face of a wife and soon to be mother stared back at him. The woman he had killed with a piano leg in his book.

Morris couldn't make himself look at her stomach, at the gaping hole the piano leg left in its wake.

"Just sign it 'To Jenny'," the woman gargled, her voice straining on ruined vocal cords. "I can't wait to read it!"

"We love Mo White!" someone from the middle of the line yelled. The voice was so degenerated, Morris couldn't tell if it was a man or a woman. Morris looked beyond Jenny to see that all of them, the entire audience—all of his fans— were dead. Not only dead. They shouldn't have existed at all. One by one, the characters of his books filed behind the other, waiting for Morris. There was Joe from the first book, who perished under the hands of a serial killer with a finger fetish; there was Mitchell Pinegrove, as naked as he had been when he died, his face bloated and discolored from lack of oxygen; there was Lyle Coleman, a bloody mess below the waist. And there were more, scores more, lined up in the darkness. Waiting for him.

Morris recoiled in disgust laced with fear so prominent, he could smell it on his own skin. The woman before him smiled wider, reaching a rotting hand toward Morris as he pushed himself away from the table. He stood to leave, to run away, but caught a glimpse of something more heinous than his "fans" in the corner of his eye. What could only be described as a thing staggered toward Morris, its legs of differing lengths and thickness. One leg was nothing more than bone from pelvis to foot. The other was covered with unblemished skin, as smooth as that of a newborn. His back was hunched over, curled like a fetus in the womb. The bones of his spine were visible in places and covered with paper-thin skin in others. His arms were almost complete. The skin on them, like one of his legs, looked healthy. His hands, however, were mashed, broken, crushed. His face was a mass of broken bones, split skin, and blood. His features were almost indistinguishable, with gaps in the skin that revealed muscle and bone. His eyes, though, were piercing. Their iridescent brown bored into Morris, chilling his very soul.

The thing said something that sounded more like a grunt than a word. Morris didn't want to hear it, didn't want to be there at all, but knew he had to. Stepping close enough that Morris could smell its breath, a scent both sweet and putrid at the same time, the thing spoke again, clearer somehow.

"Finish me!"

Morris awoke with the sound of his own screams in his ear.

"Are you all right?" The voice of a woman he didn't recognize spoke to him softly. Someone else shrieked from far away.

"A-are you all right, sir?"

Morris opened his eyes and saw the kind face of a matronly woman, hair dusted with gray and roller set like his grandmother's had been, standing in front of him. She was clutching his book to her chest. His own penetrative stare looked back at him from the back cover. She clutched the book so tightly that her knuckles were white.

Another woman rushed over with a cup of water, which Morris greedily downed. He was starting to get his bearings. He was in a bookstore, one that he'd been in before, to sign and to buy books. He was seated at a table, a stack of his books next to him, pen in hand. Okay. Made sense. He had a couple more venues on his tour for 'Fallen Angel.' He just didn't remember how he got there.

"I'm fine," Morris said unconvincingly. "I didn't get much sleep last night. That's all." The women were still worried. "The life of a horror writer, what can I say?" He smiled, but it felt wrong. Some of the people in line, mostly women per usual, chuckled but still looked at him with concern in their eyes.

Morris didn't know what was wrong with him, why he couldn't remember getting to the bookstore, coming in and sitting down, why he daydreamed such a horrible scene in broad daylight. He didn't know anything except that he wanted to sign as many books as he could and get the hell out of there.

The next woman in line smiled and handed him her book. "You can just sign that to Jenny, Mr. White. I can't wait to read it!"

Morris caught a glimpse of the title on the cover before he passed out with the smell of wet grass in his nose and a baby crying in his ears.

Jennifer's Rose, A Mo White Mystery.

\/\\|/\\|/
JACOB STREET

"Again?"

"Every damn time," Kate said, running a hand through her hair.

"Aren't there supposed to be satellites checking the routes all day long? There's like 30 of them in space, right?"

Kate shook her head because she didn't know and didn't care. All she knew was that every time they drove to Jacob Street or anywhere near it, the GPS dropped them right into the bay. It didn't matter if it was one of those old, clunky box-type GPS systems that people used to mount on their dashboards, the touchscreen ones that came with high-end cars, or an app on a smartphone.

"You'd think we'd know the way by now," Glenn said under his breath but loud enough for Kate to catch his words on the wind. And they should have. They'd traveled the same route at least four times in the past six years from the same starting point. They did the same things when they went on that route too: started later than expected, both of them procrastinating without meaning to; stopped for breakfast at some roadside dive, always saying they would try someplace new when they got in the car but ending up at the same hazy windowed joint; stopped for flowers and one of those green metal vases with the narwal-like point to dig into the ground... and ended up looking at the little icon for their car lying at the bottom of the bay.

"You'd think," Kate said and knew she didn't have to say it, but did anyway, because he didn't have to say it either, but he did. When *he* said it, it sounded like something... something she didn't like. 'We' sounded a lot like 'you' and she didn't care for it at all. She also didn't care for the haughtiness of his tone, the condescension. It reeked of accusation, chastisement. Blame.

No, she didn't like the way it sounded at all.

When *she* said it, she meant all of those things and more.

They knew the way—somewhere deep down inside, both of them did. They knew the way as much as they knew that the GPS would plop them at the bottom of the bay, driving along some unseen road in the deep. It wasn't forgetfulness... it was denial. They didn't *want* to know the way—who would ever want to commit that to memory? She would just as soon never see that place again. She could feel its fingers reaching for the back of her neck even from home.

They knew the way, but they put the address into the GPS anyway. Called the address up from memory too, their fingers typing it in without either of them even thinking about it—like it was buried in their minds, part of them... indelible. But that was all right. It had to be.

"I don't think there are that many satellites up there," Kate said, following up her snippy comeback with something less in-your-face. "Even for the US, that sounds like a lot."

"Yeah, but you'd think they'd have fixed it by now, even

if there aren't as many as I said. If there was only one up there, you'd think it would have figured out there's no road there—that it's just the fucking bay, don't you think?"

Shrill. He got to shrill a lot faster this time, Kate thought and shuddered.

"We've been coming out here for-" Glenn started but hesitated because he didn't want to say it, didn't want to tally up the years and make it real.

"I know how long we've been coming here," Kate said, cutting in and saving them both the pain.

"It's just ridiculous, that's all," Glenn said, allowing himself to be backed off the ledge.

"Technology," Kate replied offhandedly, and she knew that was the right thing to say at that very moment; it was the thing that would make it a drive instead of a trek.

Streets patterned out on a grid, curving around the water before looping over themselves, stretching, reaching, leading to somewhere else. But their car wasn't on any of them. It was there, in the middle of the green space on the screen. Kate imagined it was blinking, beeping even, like submarines do in the movies. *A watery grave for us, then, is that what this means?* Kate couldn't help but think. *Every year it calls louder, draws closer?*

"Fuck it, we're not going," Glenn said, but Kate didn't really hear it. She was too busy thinking about an underground city below the surface of the bay, some sunken town where people used to live, walk the streets, talk to neighbors. Someplace where people could sit outside their restaurants and watch the world above the surface of the water, shimmering and colorful in the light of day and ablaze with lights dotting the water at night, like stars in the sky. They were laughing down there, holding up a drink in a toast as she and her brother danced along the edge, nearer, ever closer as time moved on.

The old man waved from the side of the road, his half gloves grimed with something sticky. The plaid shirt, pulled tight against the heap of rags he wore, was tattered and dirty just like it was the year before and the year before that, his nose blinking red.

On.

Off.

On.

Off.

"Maybe it's a sign that we shouldn't go there anymore, that it's not real anymore. That none of it is." Glenn was talking, and Kate heard him. He was talking about what was real and what wasn't, what they should do and what they shouldn't, and all the while she could feel it, knew it was happening, could feel it dislodging things inside her, making loose what was once stuck firmly and she wondered how long it would take before he felt it too, before his tongue flew up from the bottom of his mouth to impale itself on his teeth, before the brackish water pooled in his throat.

"Yeah?" Kate asked, only her voice didn't sound like her, not anymore, not ever again because that person wasn't there anymore, that person's feet didn't touch the ground because the ground had been gone for centuries. She laughed and wondered who was making so much noise. Glenn turned to her, his face aglow from the beacon lighting up the deep, red blinking that showed the passage of time in beat with his heart, X marks the spot, the din that only color can bring. She laughed, and he screamed and then laughed and then cried. She told him it was enough, that he could shut up, could shut his fucking mouth finally and look at the light, look at the beacon, hear its insistent beep. And when he turned his face to it and became one with the street where he lived, the street that had been his home for many days and many nights, centuries, thousands of years when they used marble to pave the road and gold to gilt the street signs, when his face was home and his teeth pushed up into his head, she noticed something. For the first time since they were kids and he had fallen out of a tree, his leg twisted and bent beneath him so that his back was curved like a snake, and his head had landed next to hers, so close to hers that he almost broke her more, almost made her face kiss the dirt beneath the stone that had split her head open, dust to dust... For the first time since the blood dropped like tears to make wine, the red light blinked at the back of his throat again, just as it had then, lazily, but sure.

On.

Off.

On.

Off.

You are here.

\/\\\/\\\/

THE TRUTH OF THE DARK

"WHY DO YOU DO THAT? Let them go on that way?"

I could hear the disgust in his voice, but considering I couldn't even remember his name, I didn't really care.

I smirked in response, at least that's what I was trying to do, but whether it came through as the blow-off I intended it to or not is anyone's guess. Sarcasm is hard in this state; the ethereal doesn't usually lend itself to those minute details. Death has a way of flattening the features, creating a mask of one's visage such that any nuanced expression is lost. But I tried anyway.

It's frustrating, really, to be anywhere and say anything I want to at any time but not be able to make the most of it. Snark fades into a whisper, disdain wasted. If there were ever a hell on earth...

"It's cruel, you know that, right?"

This? Cruel? Clearly, he'd never met me on the other side.

"Are you sure that's the word you mean?

'Yes! I *love* you, darling. I'll never stop loving you. I-I'll always be here, waiting for the time when I can be with you again.'

He'd distracted me, and now the poor sap I had been visiting was giving away his future because he thought I was talking to him, challenging him to prove what he'd promised. Well, not me, really; he didn't know *me* from Adam, as the old folks say. He thought he was talking to his love, the one who died in a fiery wreck off the edge of town, though what town that was, I am not sure. Or did his girlfriend drown at the lake in front of hundreds of beachgoers the summer before last? I can't keep them straight. I don't even know if I ever really knew for sure, anyway.

And really, who cares?

You've seen one mournful sap, you've seen them all.

"Ok," I say to the man, only distantly realizing I had just sealed his fate as a veritable monk for the rest of his life. The notion strikes me as funny, and I smile as I back away from the precipice where he can almost see me if he peered into the nothingness that is the truth of the dark. I smiled, but only a little because he, the little shit who destroyed my evening fun, was still there, still watching me, still judging me.

"Fuck off, Dex," I said to the buzz killer. "Find something else to do."

"See? Why do you do that?"

"What?" I asked. I was growing tired of him already.

"Call me Dex," he said, deflecting. "Why do you act like I don't know anything? Why do you pretend you know more than everyone else?"

I smirked. He's hurt. Wah. Womp womp. Whatever slang his generation used to mean cry me a river, insert that.

"Oh, Dex…" I couldn't keep the condescension out of my voice.

"See? I mean, why would you call me Dexter, like I'm some kind of sociopath?"

I looked at him quizzically. Did he even know what he was talking about?

"Dexter… who?"

"Dexter. You know, from the TV show. Why would you call me his name, like I'm some kind of murderer who chops up bodies and dumps them in the ocean?"

I laughed. I couldn't help myself.

"Dexter is a character in a book, first of all, and he doesn't just chop up bodies and dump them. He has a code, a reason to do what he does, which means he's not impulsive. That also means he's a *psychopath*, genius."

"He's from TV. You can't trick me—I'm certain of it. The show came out the year I got out of high school—2006. Everyone was watching it. I had to go over to my friend's house to see it because we didn't have cable…"

2006.

2006, damn.

I don't know shit about a TV show. I read the book when it came out in 2004. By the time goofball over here was watching Dexter slice and dice on TV, I was already pushing up daisies and playing with people in the dark.

Two years is a long time.

Dex was staring.

I had zoned out.

"Well," I said too fast, like a person jerking themselves from slumber to protest that they had ever been asleep at all, "I meant Dex, short for PoinDEXter, anyway."

"Who?"

"Oh my god." I shook my head in disgust. "What do you want? Why do you keep hanging around me?" It was a legitimate question. I'd done everything I could to let him know that I didn't want him around, didn't care what he thought, hated the way he milled. And before you get goosebumps and think this is some romantic ploy, it isn't. I don't hate this dude; I literally don't think enough of him to go that far.

"I just... I don't know. I guess..."

"Jesus, spit it out already."

He looked at me like I'm rushing him. No shit, Sherlock.

"I guess I just don't understand why you act that way. You say you don't care—about anything, really, but obviously you care enough to try to help these people. You wouldn't do it every day if you didn't."

"Do *what* every day?" Why is he watching me every day? Is this dude some kind of freak? I looked at him again, closer this time. He doesn't look like he has it in him.

"Try to help people."

The woman at the séance holding the hands of a psychic so tightly, the tips of her fingers have gone numb.

The little boy looking into his grandfather's empty bedroom.

The wife crying as the water from the shower cascades down her body, so hot as to redden the flesh.

I watched them all when they thought they were alone, then answered them when they called out. I was Cliff, Vernon, and Ashton. Mary, Randolph, Wyatt, and Carol too, though I never spoke the names they called me. I was whoever they needed me to be. Because it was me they were calling to, even though their voices uttered different names, their hearts yearned for others. What they said didn't matter; their tears knew how to find me. Very much like the telephone operators from the old days knew where to route calls on their massive switchboards, their sorrow knew which button to push to reach me. I was loath to ignore it, the sweet sound of despair. I came running every time I could.

I stood idle when they flogged themselves, when they cut, when they fell to their knees. Bobby, or Ravi, or Janet wouldn't do that, wouldn't let them flay the skin or let the blood, but I do. Because I am not Bobby, or Ravi, or Janet. I am—

"Why do you go out of your way to extend kindness? Why is that a thing for you at all?"

I could ask why that isn't a thing for him, especially since he's supposed to be the anointed one here, but I guess I already know that answer. Instead, I shrugged. I don't feel like getting into this conversation with another one of the winged… not when I can hear a man sobbing somewhere in the southwest.

"What's it to you? You do you, scaring people with all those eyes and heads and whatnot, and I'll do me."

He snickered, almost laughed. That's a first.

"Is that what you see, even now?" he questioned, and I didn't much like his tone.

I hadn't taken the time to look at him, so I did then. And no, that isn't what I saw. But I also didn't see a man standing on two legs with a torso, arms, and a head covered with skin that looked anything like mine.

He read judgment in my eyes. It amused him.

"It still surprises you. That's curious."

I don't like it when they stare at me like that, like they're studying me.

I don't like that at all.

"Well, don't waste time trying to figure me out," I said,

trying to be dismissive. I'm not worth it. Bottom of the barrel. I'm not even trying to get my wings, so let me live. I'm not bothering anyone."

In the southwest, the man was crying, begging for his wife to take another breath. It was a fresh one, only minutes in, and I'm missing it. Damnit.

Dex laughed, and it was an unpleasant sound, but I guess the whole thing *was* funny in retrospect.

"Do you want to?"

"Want to what?"

"Get your wings."

I looked at him again, regarding a visage that I wasn't even sure I had the words to describe, and it was confirmed. No, I didn't.

I didn't have to say it; it just was. He saw the truth in the same way that I did.

"They are born, then they die," he started again, frustration lacing his words anew. "It is written. Why does what happens along the way concern you?"

The suffering. There is something about it, the sweet and sour smell that pain gives off, the headiness of stress. But I didn't say those things. I didn't have to. He already knew.

"They are interesting to me," I conceded.

"Because you used to be one of them?"

"There it is. And you wouldn't understand that because you weren't. Just like I can't understand why you *don't* care. I thought you were supposed to. That's what we're taught; it's one of the main things they drill into us from the beginning, but-"

"But?"

"But you show up like... this."

"Like this?"

I didn't look—not again. The idea that he might be mugging for me with that not-face was more than I thought I could take then, not when my humanity was reacting to the man in pain, his wails caressing my ears. I'm too vulnerable. Seeing the not-face's expression might scare the shit out of me.

Again.

"Put that away. You'll scare the children."

"Do not fear."

"There you go again."

"You've been here long enough to be unfazed."

I nodded, though not necessarily in agreement. Over a decade if a day."

"But time is nonexistent. I just tricked you. There is no decade. There is no day. You are not one of them anymore."

"Unless I go back."

I've been considering it. Sometimes seriously. But I'm afraid of who I would be now, of *what* I might be. I've grown accustomed to the sound of suffering. What if that came with me, tethered itself to my soul and manifested somehow? What if listening to them cry wasn't enough? What if I wanted to do something to elicit it?

"I could send you back as a flower," he said, answering the unasked question.

"My luck, I'd be a Venus flytrap."

Again, with that laugh, like sandpaper on piano strings.

"Anyway, you can't send me anywhere. Don't forget your station, buddy. You're like me in more ways that you care to admit."

"You're right—I can't. But I can suggest. You don't belong here."

No, I don't. I've known that since I got here.

The wailing man called a name out, and it wove its way to my ear from the darkness. Jenna. I thought of a response, sending it to him mind to mind so it would soothe his soul until I could break away and comfort him the way he needed.

But yeah. The one who calls himself an angel was right. I don't belong here at all.

"Leave me alone," I said, because I'd grown tired of this conversation. Again. It was the same every single time. There's nothing new—'nothing to see here, folks'. I haven't changed, haven't sprouted horns nor indifference like they expected, haven't forced my senses to shrink and mute so I could throw in and fight the good fight. It wasn't lost on me that most of the people who came here with me did so eagerly, earned their wings, and did whatever one does when they get them. But not me. Not yet. If ever.

"The rules are clear," no-face said, breaking my reverie, and I just want him to leave, to go find someone else to bother, maybe freak out an old man praying on a hill—anything but standing behind me, watching me, waiting for me to lose the will to ignore the suffering man who was damn near ripping his skin off in grief.

"Sure. That I know. Compassion has its place. Somewhere in an alley, in a dumpster, buried under fishbones and rot."

He shook his head but had no response. Good. I'd gotten a jab in, and it was a good one too. I rejoiced because it only happened every couple of years.

"You'll come to understand that one day. Perhaps when you hear your name called."

It was my turn to snicker.

"The time for that has passed, don't you think? I know

you've never been one of us, but surely you know how it works. You have to leave someone behind to have your name called. I'm safe on that front."

I felt something break off when I said that, a little barnacle falling off a rock, but I kept it from him. He didn't have to know everything.

"I am aware. It is you who are not. About a great many things, it seems."

I turned to face him, intending to demand an explanation, maybe even to suggest he remove the sarcasm from his tone as it wasn't godly, not at all, but he was gone. The man still wailed in the distance, but something in my mind turned away from him and instead looked inward to the memories I had locked away, to the living time I had tried to forget.

I looked, but saw nothing. Me in my bedroom. Me in the hallways at high school. Me at work, surrounded by gray-walled cubicles. Me at a party, drink in hand. Me in a dilapidated house, eyes hooded. Me seeing me lying dead under a park bench.

I didn't need to see that again. I hate no-face for that, though it doesn't feel like the emotion I remember. It wasn't red-hot or piercing. It just was. And that was ok.

Someone was crying. A man, but different from before. His voice was hoarse and ravaged; his tone dull and lost. He wasn't so much speaking as he was chanting. And someone was answering him. Call and response.

Back and forth.

Back and forth.

Someone was answering.

There was another.

Like me.

Pretending.

I could hear the laughter in the back of their throats as they played along, embodying the role as though running lines with the bereaved. I could hear the cruelty, could almost feel the derision beneath the false compassion he pushed through the darkness.

There *was* someone else.

Someone else... like me.

And I began to wonder how long this had been going on and who he had been talking to.

NEXT

Part Two

Sʜᴇ ᴡᴀs ʀɪɢʜᴛ.

She was right.

A million times over, seeming, but a fortnight's worth right.

The time is nigh.

I draw my sword and don't hesitate to make the cut that is required, the cut that is expected. My palm bleeds freely, and that is fine, coating her hand and drenching the floor, my blood mingling with hers spilled so many hours before.

Rusty, oxidized, topped with the fresh red of life.

Out with the old and in with the new.

I stand, and it hurts, but that is fine. I look at the ring that is now mine, the one that fits me perfectly the way no other has before, and know what needs to be done. Movement catches the corner of my eye as it had a moment ago, as it had an hour before.

White.

Small.

Like a grain of rice.

A nothing.
But it is everything in a wink.
The pyre will cleanse it all.
The fire will get them before they get her.
Long live the queen.

About the Author

L. Marie Wood is a Bram Stoker®, Golden Stake Award, and International Impact Award-winning author. She is also a MICO Award-winning screenwriter, a Rhysling and Elgin nominated poet, an accomplished essayist, and a playwright. Wood has won over 50 national and international screenplay and film awards. She has been published in groundbreaking works, including the anthologies *Sycorax';s Daughters* and *Slay: Stories of the Vampire Noire*, as well as industry staples such as the Magazine of Fantasy & Science Fiction and Nightmare Magazine and in multiple languages. Her nonfiction has been published in academic textbooks such as the cross-curricular, *Conjuring Worlds: An Afrofuturist Textbook*. She is also part of the 2022 Bookfest Book Award-winning poetry anthology, Under Her Skin, as well as Bram Stoker Award® and Shirley Jackson Award Nominee anthologies *Shakespeare Unleashed* and *Mooncalves*. Her papers are archived as part of University of Pittsburgh's Horror Studies Collection. Wood is the Vice President of the Horror

Writers Association, the founder of the Speculative Fiction Academy, an English and Creative Writing professor, a horror scholar with a Ph.D. in Creative Writing and an MFA in Speculative Fiction, and a frequent contributor to the conversation around the evolution of genre fiction. Learn more about L. Marie Wood at

www.lmariewood.com.

More From L. Marie Wood

A group of friends head out to enjoy a much-deserved night out and paintballing is on the menu. But the team they are playing against has something entirely different in mind. The friends find themselves in a battle for their lives in unfamiliar terrain against well-equipped opponents whose motivations are both irrational and lethal.

Considered, "… a true trip into the darkest depths of what mankind is capable of at its worst," by Midwest Book Review, this story is a classic tale of prey combined with slasher film "edge-of-your seat" vibes with a little modern-day relevance to keep you unsettled.

Blackened Roots is a unique collection and will be a must-have for zombie lovers. Blackened Roots takes the zombie mythos back to its roots. Drawing from a variety of cultural backgrounds, Blackened Roots imagines a world of horror and wonder where Black protagonists take center stage – as zombies, as hunters, as heroes. From a haunting recipe to sibling rivalry, a singing zombie cowboy, a slave ship, and disobedient gods stories, Blackened Roots is a groundbreaking Afrocentric zombie anthology celebrating the rich cultural heritage of the African Diaspora.

Patrick thought he knew what awaited him in the afterlife. He's learning the hard way that he was dead wrong. He is hunted by a race of giant beasts, the likes of which have never been seen by living eyes, and he is surrounded by the newly-dead from worlds beyond knowing. In this Realm, nothing and no one can be trusted.

Patrick's choices will create echoes in the world of the living. He may be the key to salvation in this Hell known as The Realm, but it may come at the cost of his family.

With his legacy on the line, can he make the right choice?

https://www.mochamemoirspress.com

About Mocha Memoirs Press

Established in July 2010, Mocha Memoirs Press's mission is to amplify marginalized voices in speculative fiction genres (science fiction, fantasy, horror). We publish bold, fearless fiction that pushes boundaries and smashes gatekeepers.

We invite you to review our catalog to review the diversity in our stories. You can access the catalog at https://www.-mochamemoirspress.com. Join our newsletter **here.**

-
You can also find us online:
Instagram - @mochamemoirspress
TikTok-@mochamemoirspress
BlueSky-@mochamemoirspress.com
Facebook facebook.com/MochaMemoirsPress

www.ingramcontent.com/pod-product-compliance
Lightning Source LLC
Chambersburg PA
CBHW020752310726
48969CB00002B/498